Endorsements

"*Born to Ride* is a story of a young girl's love for horses, lessons learned, and exciting journey through county life. Cummings has captured the essence of family life on the farm and her readers will be entertained and captivated by her story telling ability. This fun to read book is true to the lifestyle and values of those fortunate enough to have been raised in the country and will make you wish you were."

VALORIE LUND,
*Professional Thoroughbred
Race Trainer for 25 Years*

"A suspenseful tale of a little girl growing up in the country, *Born to Ride* is filled with horse adventures and lessons of farm life. I couldn't put it down, as it is adventurous, informative, and fun! Sure to thrill horsemen and country enthusiast alike, it is a must read."

JONNAVE STOKES,
*Animal Sciences,
Philomath, Oregon*

Born to Ride

Born to Ride

DR. LESLIE CUMMINGS

TATE PUBLISHING
& Enterprises

Tate Publishing is committed to excellence in the publishing industry. Our
staff of highly trained professionals, including editors, graphic designers, and
marketing personnel, work together to produce the very finest books available.
The company reflects the philosophy established by the founders, based on
Psalms 68:11,

"THE LORD GAVE THE WORD AND GREAT WAS THE COMPANY OF THOSE
WHO PUBLISHED IT."

If you would like further information, please contact us:
1.888.361.9473 | www.tatepublishing.com
TATE PUBLISHING & Enterprises, LLC | 127 E. Trade Center Terrace
Mustang, Oklahoma 73064 USA

Published in the United States of America

ISBN: 978-1-6024709-8-9
06.02.12

Born to Ride

CHAPTER 1

The Birth

THE ICY BREEZE RUFFLED their hair and stung their cheeks as the clothes they were wearing began to freeze solid. Yet the deep, cold seeping into their bones went unnoticed as the redhead and brunette waved good-bye to the last guest pulling out of the driveway. Even though she was Wendy's younger sister, Christine was her best friend and confidant, in the game of life. Together the two Newman girls shared everything…secrets, stories, adventures, and every kind of trouble young teenagers could get themselves into. They were both beginning to shake from the cold, but neither of them was willing to give in to it. The water fight had been a great end to a wildly fun birthday party. Wendy was just glad that she wasn't the one who broke the ice on the pool, as Russ, the gorgeous six foot six, 240 pound Hawaiian, threw the party goers in one after another. It was the local papers that described him as "a Greek God exploding from a box of Wheaties!" after the last basketball game. So even though the neighbor girls screamed and struggled, they secretly swooned over this handsome giant. The guys ran for their lives, but absolutely no one escaped from his watchful gaze and lightening speed. That is, no one except two cunning little girls who knew the farm like the back of their hands. Even though her body felt cold to the touch, she felt warm from all the running, laughing, and constant throwing of water. And I am sure that the wine she had snuck from her mother's glass when she wasn't looking played a slight role in adding to the warmth she felt inside. Yet, there was an even bigger reason for the heat stirring her soul… On one of her trips around the house, attempting to evade the enemy with the water jug, Wendy slipped into the barn and noticed her mare, Robin, dripping milk. That could only mean one thing… She was soon to have her long awaited foal of which she had been dreaming. And she could hardly wait!

Her dreams had been so real. She could even now see the soft fuzzy brown muzzle nickering to her from the shadows. It was to be a dark bay colt, with a star, white and bright, on his forehead. He was an elegant creature. He had a beautiful slanting shoulder, a large heart girth, and a strong rear-end that commanded attention. His incredible physique promised strength and ability, while his four dark hooves and long pasterns ensured smoothness and speed. Oh what a beauty he was! Magnificent in every way, and Wendy would call him… Shazam. Shazam would grow into a mighty stallion, which would carry her across green, grassy fields, racing from one adventure to the next. No one would be able to stop them!

Christine interrupted her thoughts with a nudge to the side, "We done good sis, they never caught us, even though we did get a little wet. Ha!" The chuckle from deep within her chest spurred pride in Wendy for having escaped time and time again from Russ's advances.

"Oh Ya!" She replied, and joined her sister in laughter. "That was so much fun! Did you see how wet Russ got? And all the other guys and gals—whew! Were they ever a mess! But wait, I have something even *more exciting* to tell you."

Then Wendy whispered the news about the mare into Christine's ear. Her already broad grin spread even larger across her little round freckled face. Yet since it was the wee hours of the morning, and both were in bad need of rest, they decided to take turns checking on the mare every hour on the hour until she began delivery. Then whoever was on watch when the water broke would run and wake the other one, so they could come watch the bundle of joy hit the ground. So heading into the house, they quickly changed into warm, dry clothes and crawled into bed for a little shuteye. Wendy jumped up onto the top bunk and Christine hit the bottom one. Since Wendy had the first check, she set the alarm for 2:00am. As she glanced back at the doorway, she noticed their pants standing where they took them off. The legs were still frozen, causing them to stiffly stand up. It was an eerie sight seeing two pairs of jeans standing by themselves in the night shadows; however, exhaustion was beginning to creep in, and she drifted off to sleep before she could even finish her prayers.

Shazam was suddenly running across the field towards her. He raced up, stopped, and spun on his haunches. Turning his little butt in her direction and swooshing his tail at her, she giggled as she watched him toss his head, and then he reared up on his hind legs. Shazam nickered at her and flashed those big brown eyes. He wanted to play! Then he spun again and bolted at a dead run.

Wendy ran after him as fast as she could. When she was out of breath, she stopped and laughed hysterically. Shazam turned and raced back towards her. When he reached her, he put his head in her chest and shoved, nearly knocking her over. Wendy gave him a gentle rub on the head and neck, as she talked to him in a sweet soft voice. She told him of the magnificent hills they were going to ride in some day. Where the green grass grew tall and full of wild flowers and the streams trickled with cool spring water. Where mountain peaks held snow year round and the evergreen and cottonwood trees grew tall and full. Where the jeep trails made perfect places to stretch your legs, and where great athletes could test their skills over jumps and other obstacles.

Sunrays hitting her face from the window jolted her awake! She glanced at the clock and it was 6:03am! Oh no! What had happened to the alarm? Was she so tired that she had slept though the buzzer? That just couldn't be! Maybe it's broken…maybe she didn't get the button all the way down…oh dear, oh dear! No time to think, Wendy scrambled from her bed trying not to wake Christine. Since she had slept in new dry clothes, she didn't have to stop to change, so quickly left the bedroom and rushed for the barn. She just had to see that baby born!

Her heart was pounding as if it would leap from her chest. When she approached the corral, right there lying on the ground was her new foal! She was so excited! And he was just the way she had seen him in her dreams. Only…only something was wrong… something was very wrong!

Her excitement quickly turned to concern as she noticed that her new foal was not moving. She then realized Robin was in a panic as the mare repeatedly nudged the still, wet little body, nickering frantically. Without being conscious of it, Wendy was over the corral fence and next to the baby in a heartbeat. The birth sack was still wrapped around Shazam's little face and body. It was too thick for his tiny hooves to penetrate and he had suffocated all alone in the night. Tears rolled down Wendy's cheeks as she tried to calm the hysterical mare. Talking to her smoothly and stroking her neck, Wendy told her how sorry she was. Then Wendy dropped to her knees beside her little dream.

Her heart was breaking. The foal she had wanted so badly… wanted all her life…the one she dreamed about…the one she was going to do miracles with—was suddenly gone. If only she had been there! If only her alarm had gone off when it was suppose to. If only she had not been too lazy to stay awake, Shazam would be alive! If only, if only…somehow the stabbing pain in Wendy's heart felt justified, and she would never, ever, forgive herself. "It's all my fault for not being there to help you when you needed me."

Crying bitterly now and ashamed that she had even been born, Wendy somehow fetched the wheelbarrow and shovel. She loaded the precious little body into the hand-driven hearse, and fending off the frantic mother, she made her way though the corral gate and down to the bottom of the field. It was there that she dug a deep hole. With every shovel of dirt, Wendy questioned the Lord. "I don't understand…Why?…Why did you take him from me? You take everything away from me that I love. First, my favorite rabbit. Then my pet goat. And now, my horse whom I have waited for all my life! I just don't understand why God." Her mind fought the turmoil that was now racing through it. Hadn't she done well, speaking well of Him? Hadn't she spent time with her friends telling them what a great friend He was, and how He made such a difference in her and her families' lives? Then why? Why take away the one thing she wanted so much? Wendy just didn't understand, and the tears continued to roll.

She laid Shazam gently into the newly dug hole, burying her heart along with her dreams on that frozen March morning. The tears would not stop running, even though her body felt numb to the bone. She had no idea how long she stood there sobbing before Christine's gentle hand touched her shoulder. No words were spoken. Christine just helped her fill in the hole with dirt, then took her by the arm and led her back to the house.

Chapter 2

Comfort

Everyday the pain in her heart got worse. Wendy repeatedly beat up on herself for not being there to save her new friend. She tried hard to put the whole ordeal from her mind, but the tears continued to fall. So she blamed herself, and blamed the alarm clock, and blamed God.

On the fifth night of no relief and no comfort, while her heart continued to ache, Wendy cried herself to sleep yet again. It was then that she had another dream. Or was it a dream? She was not sure if it was a dream or if it was real, because it felt like it was really happening.

The sun's rays were bright beyond belief and Wendy could hardly see. Then slowly her eyes adjusted and out of the light she could see her little Shazam! He was in a huge golden field with heads of grain ready to harvest and swaying softly in the breeze.

He picked his head up from eating the sweet morsels and rocked his ears forward as he noticed her standing there. Then he nickered and began trotting towards her. Somehow she could tell he was letting her know he loved her and was on his way to save her lonely heart. Oh, he was so beautiful! So precious . Wendy's heart leapt in her chest as she called out to him.

Suddenly, swooping down from the heavens came a magnificently winged stallion. Snow white in color and shiny like satin, his mighty muscles quivered as he slowed down to a gentle gallop next to her colt. A long flowing mane and even longer tail gave him a ghostly appearance as he strode beside Shazam. The two came towards her, but just before they reached where she was standing, they lifted off the ground together and galloped into the clouds. Wendy stood there staring after them until they were completely out of sight. It was then that she heard the great white stallion call back to her. In his whinny, she knew he was telling her that her baby was safe and she would see him again someday.

When Wendy awoke…or the vision was over…she still was not sure which it was, she quietly got to her knees and asked her heavenly Father to forgive her. Wendy asked Him to forgive her for blaming Him. For not trusting Him to do what was best for her Shazam. She then thanked Him for his wonderful loving care, and began to softly sing songs of love and thanksgiving to Him from a heart that was beginning to mend. When Christine came in to get her for breakfast, she could tell that Wendy was somehow comforted. Christine didn't ask her any questions, for which Wendy greatly appreciated. She decided to keep her newest dream to herself, at least for the time being. Wendy just wasn't ready to share it with anyone—even Christine. Yet from that day forward, she understood that her Shazam was with her Father in heaven and that she would see him again sometime in the future. The tears stopped, even though she still felt somewhat responsible. Wendy knew the Lord had forgiven her and she would someday get to see her beautiful colt in heaven. Shazam would be waiting for her.

CHAPTER 3

Life Goes On

DAYS FLEW INTO WEEKS, and weeks flew into months. As the time went by, Wendy's heart slowly healed. Christine and Wendy stayed busy on the small farm with all the animals. Not only did they care for the animals, they also learned valuable lessons about dressing animals for food and breeding hearty stock. Their mother taught them most things. She taught them about raising food for the animals, as well as for others. They learned about different food sources including meat, eggs, grasses, vegetables, herbs, berries, fruits and the like. Not only how to raise them or gather them, but also how to prepare them for meals and long-term storage. The lessons were many and exciting, and the girls never got tired of them.

The farm animals quickly grew to include fifteen horses, seven cows, nineteen goats, one-hundred sheep, twenty-four chickens, and more rabbits than you could count! Every animal had a name and special place prepared just for them. The girls loved them all!

The goats were a special tug at the heart. Lynette started with Heidi, Wendy started with Mabel, and Christine started with Classy. The girls quickly learned about the different breeds of goats—Saanens, French Alpines, Nubians, Toggenburgs, and Lamanchas to name a few. Each had their special characteristics. Some were born only white, others were born only brown, and some were born multiple colors. Some provided heavy butterfat in their milk, while others provided large quantities. Some were ear-less, some had roman noses and long floppy ears, and some fainted when frightened. All were friendly and thought they were born a person! Ha! However, when the babies started arriving, even Mom and Dad got hooked. They would follow you anywhere. They would play King of the Mountain, ride on your lap, or nibble on your shirt. They were just happy to be with you and wanted to join in on what ever it was you were doing.

Christine and Wendy took several of the small herd to the 4-H and State fairs where they won all kinds of blue ribbons. The girls also learned that goat's milk was naturally homogenized, and that it had a small curd, which made it not only healthy, but also easy to digest. This made it very attractive for babies and older folks, and they sold a lot of it. They learned how to breed for milk quality and joined a farm program, which tested, graded, and monitored each goat's milk for a year. Soon they had a Grade-B dairy and earned a fair name for breeding quality goats. People started hunting them down for breeding stock and before long they were selling babies all over the Northwest. The girls even sold some as far away as Fairbanks, Alaska. And when it came time to finally sell out their entire herd, the last goat brought over three thousand dollars!

The sheep were another great learning experience that they made a fair amount of money from. The family not only earned money from selling the wool, they earned from the lamb crop as well. Christine and Wendy learned which breeds produced the best meat lambs and which ones were the better wool producers. They learned how to sheer their own sheep and how to grade the wool. They never did learn how to clean and spin the wool for yarn though, as they never had the time for that part. Instead the girls learned all the business aspects, such as when and where to sell their stock, government subsidies, and the like.

They started with twelve nice crossbred ewes that Christine had talked a neighboring rancher out of. Then, she purchased a beautiful Suffolk ram whom they called Zeb. Zeb was not only strong and beautifully built, he produced lots of twins, which meant a much larger lamb crop. The girls also made several trips to the local auction for culls that other farmers were removing from their herds. These "culls" often had problems associated with them, such as mastitis, worms, bad teeth, or other such things. The farmers didn't want to mess with them and that is why they were sold cheap. Yet, with a lot of careful attention and love, they would soon be healed of their ailment and would be ready to breed. The girls had learned these lessons previously on the farm, before Cora's accident.

During lambing season, Christine and Wendy would sleep in the barn and watch babies born nearly every night. They would haul out their sleeping bags and make a bed on top of the alfalfa hay pile. Sometimes they would make a small fort out of the hay to make the stay a little more interesting. The girls would sip on hot chocolate and eat snacks, which never failed to bring the cats around.

When the ewes began to lamb, they would crawl down and watch from a short distance away. If a ewe needed assistance, one would move up to her side and help with the birth. This usually meant pulling an extra large lamb or assisting with multiple births. There were always several sets of twins and triplets born, and once there were even quintuplets! One night the girls had a young ewe that tried and tried to lamb, but that wasn't progressing. So Christine reached inside to see what the problem was, only to discover a tail! The ewe was too small inside to turn the baby around, so they had to pull it out backwards. When the baby stood and took her fist suck from mama's udder, the girls decided to call her Backward Betty.

Every once in a while, a ewe would not accept a lamb or would die shortly after birthing. And sometimes dogs would get into the field and kill several mothers. Regardless of the cause, they would have to care for the babies. Yet, it was a blast feeding the bummer lambs by bottle! The girls would fill coke bottles with milk and put a nipple on top. Then they would feed as many babies as they could at one time, often holding one bottle in each hand and one between their knees. The lambs would *baah* at them, run for the bottle, bump it with their little noses, and wag those little tails. If the girls weren't careful they could knock them over! Quickly and efficiently the little guys would suck down an entire bottle of milk so fast that one could hardly believe their eyes!

When the lambs were a week old, the girls would put ear tags in their ears for identification and place their names in a logbook. They would then cut their tails short and weather the males. Only a few outstanding males got to stay rams for future breeding. As the lambs got older, the girls separated them into their own field and fed them grain and alfalfa. Soon they would grow big enough to sell at market or move into the herd. Since it only took a year before a ewe lamb was old enough to breed, and it only took five months for the ewes to have their babies, the herd grew fast. It wasn't long before the family had over a hundred sheep on the place.

All of the sheep were named. There were the fun names like Malikatriky and Felekadonki. There were silly names like Stuff-a-gut and Starvena, Old Blind Hannah or Simple Susie. And then there were normal names like Clementine, Lady Ellen, and Speck-les. The boys were named after the boys in the neighborhood and the girls took special pleasure in teasing them about that. There was Matt-the-Meat, Kockeyed Kenny, Yummie Jimmie, Little Mean Phil, and Lazy Lester to name a few.

The chickens provided a different kind of fun. There were some of the normal breeds such as Rhode Island Reds, Cornish, and Leghorns. Then there were the specialty breeds like Araca-nas, Polish (which were nicknamed "hippy chicks"), Bantams, Buff Cochins, Silver Laced Wyandotte, and Jersey Black Giants. The girls sold fresh eggs of all different colors and occasionally sold a fryer or two. Each of the chickens were named, but Bicken and Lucky were the favorites. Lucky, because she always seemed to escape danger—skunks, foxes, and other varmints that tried to steal eggs and kill chickens, and Bicken, because Christine had hand raised her and she thought Christine was her mother.

The rabbit portion of the farm started with two very prolific females, Brown Betty and Kick-a-poo Joy Juice. Both had between eight and twelve bunnies at a time and they had a new batch nearly every month. In fact sometimes, a new batch would arrive before the girls could wean the batch before! Like the sheep and goats, the girls learned as they went along. Christine and Wendy learned about the different breeds and which ones were good for fur, which were good for meat, and which were good for selling as pets. They purchased a couple of lop-eared does and some more meat rabbits. Then they picked up a few exotic breeds such as Rex, Dutch, and Siamese to add to the collection. The girls built their own cages and fed the rabbits mostly from the family garden. In next to no time however, they were out of cages and water dishes, so Christine and Wendy decided to turn all but the exotics loose.

The rabbits settled in nicely. They dug little dens in the dirt and kept the grass edges in the yard trimmed. Soon new additions would be seen hopping around the backyard and throughout the barn area. The girls lost count of how many rabbits there were and didn't realize how much they had multiplied until Mitch made them catch all of them after the rabbits nearly destroyed the garden. There were over a hundred fryer-size rabbits in the little red goat shed when the girls got done catching! That did not count the adults or the little babies. Although they never really knew how many rabbits had been born on the place, because a tomcat who loved to catch and eat them also lived on the farm. The cat weighed over twenty pounds and would bring down rabbits larger than himself. The girls couldn't break him of it, so they tried to give him away. But "Old Tom" kept coming back. One time the family even dropped him off at a friend's house over forty miles away! And Tom still came back. Finally, they gave up and sold the remaining rabbits.

Then there were the cows. Or "cattle," since there were both cows and steers. No bulls thankfully. Isis, Gretel, and Deadly were the cows that raised calves and produced milk. While Sneaky Pete, Question Mark, Roast Beef, and Sirloin were the steers. I guess you can tell which ones were intended for the dinner table.

Christine and Wendy didn't embrace the raising of cattle like they did the other animals, as the cattle were so big and hard to work with. They didn't have many brains according to Christine, and they could really hurt if careful attention was not paid. Even then Wendy got side kicked many times by an irritated cow, butted, run over, and nearly gored.

Deadly was calving and Wendy could see feet. So she decided to sneak up for a better look. Only Deadly had other plans and when Wendy got closer than the old cow thought she should, she charged. Her horns were long and stuck straight out, thus her name; however, Deadly had not actually charged anyone before. So Wendy ran like the devil was chasing her and leaped up onto the top rail of the corral fence just as Deadly's horns hit. Ka-Wham!!! If she had not been slower than normal due to the calving, she would have got Wendy for sure! While Wendy let the thump thump of her heart settle down, Cora came out to see why she was on the fence. Wendy recapped the last few moments and shared that she was afraid something was wrong with the birth, so Cora stayed with Wendy for a bit watching from a distance. When it was clear that Deadly was indeed in trouble, Cora called the vet for assistance—something they rarely did. The vet came quickly but it still took him, Cora, and a come-a-long to get the huge calf out. When it was clear that the calf was nursing and healthy, and the cow fully recovered, Cora drove Deadly and her youngster to the auction. One of the main rules of the farm was no dangerous animals.

So, in addition to the tough and sometimes dangerous work, there really wasn't much profit in raising cows. They had just a few milk customers, butter in the fridge, and excellent beef in the freezer. Yet, there were some fun times with the cows, like the time

Christine decided to put a saddle pad on Gretel and ride her, or the time they jumped Isis in the back of the pickup with no racks or sides to take her to a nearby farm so the vet could remove her horns. But mostly the cows didn't do much for the girls. Their hearts were with the horses...with that thought years past came suddenly racing to the forefront of Wendy's mind. Back to the very beginning, and back to where she first gained her deep desire and love for horses.

CHAPTER 4

The Place

IT WAS A VERY DIFFERENT place and a very different time. But to Wendy's young mind, it was like yesterday. She could remember so clearly her first glimpse of the farm that sent her heart racing. Among several large oak trees sat a dilapidated old farmhouse with a wrap-around covered porch. She thought it was white in color, but wasn't really sure, as the paint reflected years of wear and some of the color simply melted into the wood siding. The house was so old, it looked as if it might fall down at any moment and a similar looking detached garage greeted them as they pulled into the driveway. The front and back yards had old wooden rails separating the property from the road and neighboring fence. Amongst the rotting wood were huge clumps of weeds mixed within old beds of daffodils, irises, tall tiger lilies, and dahlias, as well as various flowering shrubs to which Wendy could not readily identify. Some antique farm equipment lay in pieces throughout the flowerbeds and yard in what seemed like an intentional display.

To her right were two old barns in even worse shape than the house and garage. These old wooden structures had lost any resemblance of paint years ago. Now only bare grey wood scarred by years of abuse and full of holes, were visible. The barns were surrounded by a rotted cedar fence post with several strands of broken rusty wire. A similar looking fence was wrapped around the hay fields, which appeared to run for miles. Clusters of scattered oak trees could be seen throughout the acreage. Dips and hollows full of weeds and scrub brush added to the rustic look that greeted them. There were no creeks or ponds, and no neighbors that you could see in any direction. Off in the distance one could view the hills that slowly turned into rather large mountains. Mother had claimed it was paradise, but to Wendy's ten-year old eyes, it looked nothing like it.

Whistling Mitch climbed out of the car and stretched. "We're here!" He yelled. Then he turned his attention to the girls. "Are you going to just sit there or do I have to come around and pull you out?" Wendy, Christine, and Lynette all giggled as they cautiously slid from the back seat. "Boy it feels good to get out of that car!" He said. Cora chimed in,

"You can say that again. I don't think I'll be able to sit for a bit after that marathon drive we just had." She was about to comment further, but the haggard look Mitch shot her, told her it might be best to hold her tongue for the moment.

"Yahoos" and "Yippees!" flooded the courtyard as five Tendicks children ran towards them. "They're here! They're here!" Anna, Caleb, David, Joshua, and Nina kept yelling. Stepping out onto the front porch were Aunt Betty, Uncle Adrian, Grandpa and Grandma Brewer, and Maxine Taylor. "You must be worn out" Betty said. "We were expecting you hours ago. Come on in and get a bite to eat. We've got beef stew and homemade rolls waiting." With that Cora and Lynette headed up the steps. But Wendy and Christine didn't want to go inside just yet, as they knew there would be long hours of jabbering the night away with a bunch of old stuffy adults. Plus they had been bound up in that car for just too many hours. So Christine turned to Mitch and sweetly asked, "Daddy, can we please take a look around first? Then we promise to come in and eat." Mitch replied, "Sure my little princesses, but don't take too long, as we wouldn't want your food to be spoiled." In a blink of an eye, the girls turned and ran for the largest of the old barns, as fast as their little feet would carry them.

Unbeknownst to them, they were followed by David, Caleb, and Joshua. From a distance the boys watched and plotted. You see, when the Tendicks boys got together, they were troublemakers. And they were scheming. After all, this was their place wasn't it? At least they had overheard their parents discussing how they had planned to buy some of the land from the Newmans to build a new home on. So the property and all that it contained was fair game as far as they were concerned, and they didn't want to share—especially with girls!

Wendy and Christine had found and entered a doorway that led them into the huge wooden structure, which now loomed above them. Stacks of old grass hay filled the great expanse, leaving only a small isle-way to travel through. "This must have been here forever," Christine exclaimed looking up towards the ceiling. "Whew! It must go all the way to the heavens! And look how dusty it is. Do you think it's any good?"

"Dunno" said Wendy. "Maybe we should climb up for a better view." With that Wendy and Christine started crawling up the musky and sometimes loose hay bales. A large barn owl swooshed by them irritated at having been disturbed. It landed on a huge wooden beam that crisscrossed near the roof. "Wow! Will you look at that!" Christine cried with eyes scanning the great structure. "Hey, we could build a fort…just look at all these bales!"

"Yah! And we can make it our special hideout," chimed Wendy. "Maybe we can get some of the other kids to help out…then we could have a slumber party…maybe even have hot cocoa and animal crackers! That would be so cool…"

It was then that they heard snickers coming from somewhere below them. "Who's there?" Wendy cried. Complete silence awaited them. "I don't want to have to come down there and get you!" she yelled. Laughter erupted from the boys, as they could no longer contain themselves. "Go ahead if you think you're manly enough! You wusses!" was Caleb's snide reply. Wendy's face turned bright-red and she stiffened. Then she started to climb down to face the intruders.

Christine quickly reached over and grabbed her arm. Whispering she said, "Wait… Wait a minute… It's just the boys and they don't know us very well yet. Give them a little time and they will become friends…" she paused. "And maybe even allies…" Wendy thought about it, and then agreed. So she sat down beside Christine on the soft bales. After a minute or two, Wendy said rather smart like, "Don't you boys want to come up here and meet us? You might even find that you like us. Besides, we are going to build a fort."

Taking only a minute to think about it, the three boys scrambled up to where the girls were. After sizing each other up they decided that a fort was much more interesting than warring right now, so they called a truce. After all, maybe these girls weren't quite the sissies they had thought. Besides…they *loved* forts! And who knows…maybe allies would be good…besides…they still had Anna, Nina, and Lynette to pick on, not to mention the other neighborhood kids that showed up from time to time.

It didn't take long before the five of them were working together as a team. One would pull bales out of the way, while another would strategically stack. Someone else grabbed pieces of wood and old boards that could be used for supports and hauled them up top. Another helped hold things in place while someone tied hay ropes together to prevent cave-ins. Soon the crew was covered in hay dust and dry grass, but they had carved out a large area approximately ten feet wide, by fifteen feet long and eight feet deep. With a little more work they had tunnels leading to and from the large room—which was now covered on top with bales and loose hay. When they heard a cry coming from the house telling them it was time to eat, there was little evidence of the now hidden fort to be seen from an outsider. So they made a pact not to tell anyone and they all promised to meet there again tomorrow afternoon. Later they would add to the structure until they had an entire system of tunnels and rooms running throughout the vast pile in the barn. Now it was time to make their way to the house for dinner.

A race to the front porch made the trip across the field much more interesting. Caleb had reached the door first, and when he swung it open, an aroma of beef stew filled the air. Getting a good whiff of the tantalizing odor, the girls realized just how hungry they were and quickly took a seat at the table. The day's journey and recent work effort had taken its toll on their bodies and now they needed nourishment. As meals were served, Christine, Wendy, Caleb, and David—now fast friends—began shoveling the delicious dinner into their mouths. Wendy barely took time to look around as she satisfied her appetite. Yet when she excused herself from the table, she couldn't help but notice that the inside was in not much better shape than the outside had been. Mentally noting that everyone had a whole lot of work ahead of them, she followed the other girls to a tiny bedroom where she found a sleeping bag laid out on the floor. By the time her head hit the pillow, she was already drifting off to sleep.

CHAPTER 5

Settling In

WHEN SHE OPENED HER eyes the suns rays were already blasting through the window. She had shared a room with Christine, Lynette, Nina, and Anna. They had been packed in like sardines, but she didn't really mind as it was almost like camping out. Now she sat up and looked around. Nina and Anna had already gone and her two sisters slept soundly on the bed just above her. Trying not to wake them, she decided to find her bag and get dressed.

Glancing around for her bag, she realized the room was lit up by sunlight streaming in from a window at the back of the room. It had a large wooden frame wrapped around it, with a frame that didn't close all the way down, leaving about a one-inch gap where fresh air freely entered. Although the air smelled sweet and Wendy welcomed it, she wondered how the bugs and mosquitoes stayed out.

A door at the other end of the room wasn't much better. The gap beneath it was almost two inches and a huge crack ran all the way down the side where it hung on rusty hinges. The walls of the room were a light pinkish-orange color and were decorated with posters of horses, rodeos, and cowboys. Wooden shelves had been hastily installed about a foot from the ceiling and ran the full length of the room above her head. The shelves held shirts, sweaters, jeans, and other clothes, as well as, several little horses of different types and colors. Wendy loved horses so this sight was very pleasing to her.

Hand made bunk beds ran from one end of the room to the other and down the left side. The beds came out past the middle of the room, leaving only a small space to walk, or in her case, to lay a sleeping bag down. That is where she was laying before she pulled herself up, and placed her back against the sidewall to view her surroundings.

Still scanning for her bag, she noticed Barbie dolls, doll clothes, puppets, and building blocks of some sort, tossed in the corner. There was no dresser or furniture other than the beds. Nothing else would fit in this room anyway, she was thinking when she saw a long dark furry thing swoop under the closed door then disappear. What was that! She said to herself as she yanked her knees up towards her chest. She was still a bit sleepy, so perhaps she just imagined it. Then it came again. Next thing she knew, she was up off the floor and onto the bunk bed with Christine and Lynette. "What is that!" she said, nearly hysterical and shaking the bed and waking Christine. "What....?" said Christine as she tried to remove the sleep from her eyes.

"Look! There it is again!" Wendy said with slightly more control as she pointed to the bottom of the door. Together the girls watched as a dark furry thing swooshed under the door again. This time Wendy had gained her senses and she grabbed a wooden stick horse that had been standing next to the bed to use as a weapon. As she approached the door ready to eliminate the critter, she got a better look. It was then that she realized the furry thing wasn't a rat or mouse after all, but a cat's leg! The cat was trying to reach a piece of pancake that had fallen on the floor and was just out of reach behind the door. She couldn't believe what she saw and she began to giggle. When Christine joined her, Lynette began to stir. "Shut up and go back to sleep!" Lynette cried. It was then the girls heard footsteps approach from outside. The furry leg disappeared and the door slowly opened.

Nina, with her blond hair and large blue eyes, stood gazing at them in wonder while holding a large dark calico cat in her arms. Her six-year old mind did not understand the laughter, so she mumbled something about pancakes being on the table. Christine reached over and shook Lynette until she was fully awake. Then in their pajamas, all four of them headed to get breakfast.

Before they reached the table, they could smell the hot butter and syrup, and Wendy's stomach began to rumble with hunger pains. When they entered the dining area they were greeted by a couple of empty chairs with pretty white plates, orange juice glasses, and two large stacks of dollar-sized pancakes. Wendy turned to glance at Christine and Lynette behind her, as if to say—now this is more like it. When she looked back at the table she discovered the pancake plates were empty! Even though Cora was plopping the tasty morsels on the platter as fast as the skillet would cook them, the boys were eating them just as fast! Wow! They can really hold their pancakes! And Caleb would quickly grab every crumble or piece that was left! Just when Wendy thought the rest of them might starve, Cora added another large batch to the platter. Even though Wendy didn't get any of those either, she knew the sweet cakes would keep coming until all were full. So rather than fight for the food, she waited patiently with the other girls until the boys had their fill and left.

With the boys gone, there was more room at the table and the conversation much more pleasant. Not to mention the food much easier to reach. "Mom," asked Lynette. "Do all of us girls really have to share a room together?" "I mean, how long will we have too share?" "I hear the boys have two rooms and there are only three of them."

"Now I don't want to hear any of your fussing Lynette," Cora replied. "The boys are sharing with Grandpa too, as Grandma's snoring keeps him awake and she can't sleep on the couch. We are all sharing and making do until we can remodel and build a new section onto the house. The new section will have a couple more bedrooms, another living room, and a new bathroom. But even then you will still need to share a room with a couple of the girls. That is until we are ready to build a new home. Remember, we are all in this together and that means share and share alike." Lynette pouted a little, but settled down when the next round of pancakes came.

"Now, I want to get us organized," said Cora. "As you can see we have a very full house and everyone must pull their share. So I have made out a list of chores, and we will take turns doing them. For right now, Lynette you and Anna will help out in the kitchen with cooking and cleaning. Wendy, you and Christine will feed the cows and horses…" That was all that Wendy heard. Just the mention of horses sent her heart racing, and she couldn't get away from the table fast enough. Scrambling into the bedroom she threw on her jeans and boots. Then she was out the door and on her way to the barn with Christine hot on her heels behind her.

Why hadn't Mom mentioned the horses before? "Wendy... Wendy!" Cora was behind her. "Now don't you go and get in too much of a hurry. I haven't even finished telling you your duties yet. Besides I don't want you to get too close to those horses!" That stopped the girls in their tracks. Turning back around to face their mother, she continued. "They are a bit wild and not yet broke to ride. That is why I got such a good deal on them. The small red mare is in foal to a nice POA stud with a baby at her side, and the buckskin mare is coming three. I plan to break them as time permits. I might even start the young mare later this week and you may watch *if* you're good and get all your chores done." Then a smile crossed her face and she said to go ahead and go take a peek—but reminded her and Christine not to get too close.

They had missed the horses the night before because they were penned up in the little barn and not the big one. As Christine and Wendy got closer they could see the little barn had a whole set of corrals. The system of wooden chutes, panels, and gates allowed for maneuverability of several head of large livestock, cattle or horses. The corral was old, but solid and there was evidence of recent repairs. Inside the door they discovered three box stalls along the side and a tack area. A tack area held a small amount of prime alfalfa hay and grain, a couple of halters, several ropes, and an older leather bridle and saddle. At the other end was a large open area with removable wooden panels separating it from the stalls. The open area allowed the horses freedom to come and go from the barn to the corral though a four-foot by eight-foot doorway.

A set of wooden stairs led to a full loft above. In the loft, the girls found some old dusty hay, probably from the same harvest that the big barn held. There were slots in the loft floor that allowed one to toss hay down to the feeders below. A rather large white barn owl occupied the center beam at the very top, which also appeared to hold a nest. "So this is where you live," Christine whispered as she bent down to examine the large clumps of owl remains that had fallen onto the floor from above. Looking up at the owl again she said, "You must be a good mouser." Crawling back down the wooden steps the girls went in search of the horses.

Turning towards the barn door at the other end, Wendy called softly. "Come on babies…come on." They could hear the horses shuffle around, but even after a few minutes there was no sign of them. So Wendy crawled though the wooden panels and headed slowly for the doorway to get a better look. "Remember what Mom said," Christine spoke cautiously. "We aren't supposed to get too close as they are wild!"

"I know, I know, but don't you think we can at least get a peek?" Wendy replied still creeping towards the open doorway. That was all the encouragement Christine needed as she too hopped through the panels and followed her sister. As they reached the other end, they cautiously peered out…

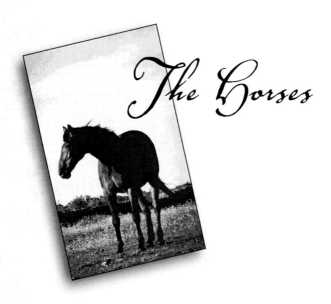

CHAPTER 6

The Horses

A FURRY RED FANNY WITH a gigantic belly attached and tail dragging the ground was the first sight to greet them. A little yellow-gold colt trimmed in black was lying sprawled out on his side as he slept next to his very pregnant mother. A light buckskin face with huge brown eyes was facing them, and she flipped her head up and snorted when she spotted the two heads peeking around the corner. This caused the red mare to jump forward and the sleeping foal to leap to his feet. Soon all parties were gazing at each other in surprise as the morning sun beat down from above.

Talking in a soft voice, Wendy tried to sooth the now alert and nervous horses. They seemed to respond, but were in no way interested in coming any closer. When the girls stepped out into the sunlight, the mares bolted for the other end of the corral. "Whew! This is going to take a lot of work!" Wendy said.

"You can say that again!" cried Christine. "I sure do like that little guy though…isn't he a cutie?"

"Oh yeah…and I'll bet those quick reactions mean these horses can get up and really go if they want to!" Wendy was sure that these horses could out- run just about anything in a pinch. And right now she and Christine were their pinch. At least they couldn't go very far—as the entire corral gates were closed. When the girls started walking towards the mares, the horses began to panic. They backed themselves into a corner and turned to face the approaching intruders weaving slightly from one front foot to the other as if ready to bolt at any moment. When the girls stopped, the older red mare began shaking her head and laying her ears back in warning. The other two horses were trying their best to squeeze in behind the dominant mare and hide. "Wait!" Christine cried. Then she disappeared back through the doorway of the barn. Wendy quietly waited. She kept glancing between the horses and the barn door for what seemed like forever before Christine reappeared. In her hands was a small amount of alfalfa. "Good thinking sis!" Wendy said as she let Christine creep past her with the offering of peace in her outstretched hand.

More snorts and stomping of the feet froze Christine in her tracks. Then, some more sweet-talking calmed the nervous horses. After a few minutes of everyone standing very still, and the gentle voices filling the air, the younger buckskin mare made a small step towards the hay. Sniffing the wind as if to see if it were really worth the risk, the young mare kept one eye on Christine, and one on the offering. More snorts and a few inches closer she came. Shaking her head up and down as she slowly approached, the young mare watched Christine for any reaction or movement. None came. So she got a little braver and took a few more steps forward. After a few more tests, she walked right up to Christine and began munching on the delicious green stuff. But the red mare and her foal would have nothing of it. They stayed backed tightly into the corner and looked on with wild eyes as the buckskin ate. When the food was all gone, Christine slowly turned and started back towards Wendy. To her surprise, the young mare followed.

Heartened by her reaction, the two girls headed into the barn for more alfalfa. This time the young mare came all the way into the barn for her goodies. After a few minutes, the red mare and foal were peeking through the barn doorway watching the other mare eat from the girl's hands. But the red mare and foal still would not enter the barn. So the girls left the open pen area and went over to the other side where the stalls and tack room were. They continued to talk in soft tones as they watched the red mares ears flicker back and forth. She was listening. After a bit more time, she cautiously entered with her baby following closely behind. When she spotted the two girls across the barn, she ran over to take the food away from the younger mare. It was clear that she was the boss, as the younger mare quickly moved aside leaving her delicious treasure.

The girls decided to name their new friends. Let's call the light buckskin mare Champagne," said Christine "and the little guy Mike."

"And the red mare Robin," Wendy chimed in. "The red, red, Robin, goes bob, bob, bobbin along…" she sang. The two were so proud of themselves. The buckskin was looking around for more food, and when she spotted the two girls talking over near the stalls. She softly nickered. That was the cats meow to Christine and she quickly brought her some more hay. With that, the girls knew they had made great progress and decided to call it enough for the day. They didn't want to push their luck and cause a problem down the road, so they headed over to the big barn to check on last night's endeavors. But not before they agreed to keep this secret to themselves. As they had every intention of breaking those wild horses in the weeks to come, and no one would be the wiser.

After a couple of hours in the big barn, the girls felt as though they had made enough "fixes" to the growing fort. They were surprised to discover that someone else had added another complete room and placed an old wooden cable roll on its side in order to provide a table of sorts. Two stuffed pillows worked as chairs and added a nice touch to the now very cozy room. The girls assumed it had been the boys, so they did some more digging for treasures themselves. They found some old wooden boards that would work well for shelves, an old blanket that they could use to cover loose hay for a bed, and a couple of empty tuna cans that would make nice candleholders. Now if they could just get a couple of candles and a book of matches…

On their way back to the house they found Cora and Betty on opposite sides of a large Guernsey cow milking. The five-gallon bucket was nearly full and the cow's udder looked as if they hadn't even started the milking. "Well Betty, I don't know if it's me or this darn cow. But ole' Dagmar here is going to kill us all if she continues to give us eight plus gallons a day. It's way more than we need and my hands just won't take it! Have you thought about getting her a calf?" Betty replied. A surprised look crossed Cora's face.

"Great idea! I'll head over to the auction on Sunday and find us a good one." Noticing the two girls, Cora told them they still had their chores to do. "Run into the house and look at the list on the kitchen sink. If you have any questions come back and check with me, otherwise—get to it!" Adrian and Mitch chose that moment to come up for a cool drink and lunch. But within seconds they were swapping places with the ladies and milking into a fresh bucket.

Following Cora, Betty, and the bucket of milk into the house, Christine and Wendy went to check the list. As they watched their mother and Betty pour the bucket of milk into a large stainless steel pot with a strainer attached, and then into glass jars, they went over their newly assigned duties. When the milk was safely stored into the extra fridge on the back porch, Cora asked if they were hungry and began making sandwiches. Still examining the list, Wendy wanted to know if brushing the horses could be part of her responsibility. "Well, you would still have to do the laundry and take out the garbage. And Christine would still have to do the vacuuming. Plus you both have to help in the garden. But if you really want to, I guess I could let you brush them on *one* condition—no trying to catch them or brush them without me, understood?"

"Understood!" replied Wendy a little too enthusiastically.

"I mean it Wendy. Absolutely no messing with those horses without me there with you! And don't forget the cow and her calf."

"What calf?" Wendy asked.

"The one I am going to get her on Sunday" Cora replied.

"Ok" and with that Wendy grabbed her sandwich and ice tea, and headed back outside. Whistling she made her way to the huge oak tree in the front yard and sat in its cool shade.

Christine joined her shortly thereafter. "I had to find out more about the new calf," she said as she sat down. "I had to get my two cents in for a girl, because I know we will raise any males to eat. Wow… it sure is nice out here."

"Yes it is, isn't it? And since we need the meat real bad, I'll bet she brings home a boy calf." As they ate, they watched Cora carry a plate full of sandwiches and a pitcher of ice tea out to the two men just getting off the milk stools. Another five-gallon bucket had been filled to the brim. "She sure does give her share of the goods, doesn't she" Mitch said standing up and removing the bucket from the cow's underbelly. Cora just smiled as she took the bucket from him and went back into the house.

As Mitch and Adrian each grabbed a sandwich and a glass of tea, Caleb and David arrived. The food disappeared quickly as the guys sucked down their meals. "Well I guess we had better head back out. That fence isn't going to get finished if we keep lollygagging down here all day," said Adrian.

"Yeah, I think we can finish the south side if we really get after it," replied Mitch. Then the crew ambled back towards the hay field chattering away about all the fence work left to do.

"I guess we don't have to wonder what the boys will be doing for the next few days," Wendy commented.

"That's very good news..." piped up Christine. "...cause now we can work in the barns without fear of getting caught." Wendy smiled and nodded in agreement as she took another bite.

When the girls were done with their lunch they went inside to attend to their chores. There they found Nina and Anna at the kitchen sink peeling potatoes, and Lynette making a mess with what appeared to be a cheesecake. "Do any of you know where the vacuum cleaner is kept?" asked Christine.

"What on earth do you need that for?" Anna asked.

"Just look at these floors! There's no carpet so a big broom will work. In fact it will do a much better job of getting all the dirt out of these large cracks."

"Ok. Then where do I find the broom?" asked Christine.

"It's in the pantry closet in the back." Nina said pointing her finger at the door to her right that led to a back porch. She then turned her attention back to her half peeled potato. Christine headed for the back porch to find the broom. "That's where the laundry is too," Nina said this time without removing her focus from her work. Wendy jumped to catch up with Christine.

With the door closed behind them, Wendy started gathering up all the dirty clothes. "I guess maybe we should have been helping sooner," she commented to her sister. "Maybe we need to spend a little more time getting to know Anna and Nina." She started a load of clothes while Christine retrieved the broom.

"All in good time" was all Christine said, then she left the room to go sweep floors.

Wendy was careful to remove the rugs and shake them before placing them back onto the hard wood. Then she sorted the rest of the whites from the colors while Christine finished her floors. Christine came by her a few minutes later with a small dish of tuna for the cat—whom she now knew as Rainbow—then returned to the kitchen to talk to the other girls.

While they visited, Wendy went throughout the house emptying the garbage pails into a large black bag. She then delivered the garbage to the cans just outside the back porch. When Wendy finally reentered the kitchen, she heard loud noises coming from the living room. She assumed it was just Cora and Betty who were in the back nailing down some loose wooden boards. Then Cora yelled for the kids to pipe down just as a huge crash came from the living room. It sounded to Wendy like the whole house was falling down! The girls all made a mad dash for the living room.

There in the middle of the floor was Dagmar the cow. Her feet had gone clear through the rotten floorboards and her belly was now rubbing them. Betty ran towards her waving the hammer still in her hand and yelling, "Shoo! Shoo!" When the cow didn't budge, Cora tried to get her feet back onto solid boards. Dagmar still didn't move an inch as she watched them flit around her. It took Cora and Betty several tries to get the cow unstuck and back outside. "Who left the door open?" Cora cried as she came back in. Then her and Betty looked at the mess and broke into fits of laughter. Soon the entire crew was in hysterics, holding their sides with tears running down their cheeks.

"What in the world are we going to tell the men?" Betty asked meekly.

"The truth!" Cora replied. Which brought even more laughter.

CHAPTER 7

Evening Excursions

AROUND DUSK THE GUYS came dragging their tired bodies into the dining room for dinner. If they noticed the floor, no one said anything. A hot meal was placed before them and after the blessing everyone ate in silence. It had been a long day and all were exhausted. "I think I'll hit the sack early tonight," said Mitch. "It's going to be another full day on the fences tomorrow."

"I'm going to head to bed too," said Adrian. With that he raised himself from his chair and headed off to his and Betty's bedroom. Betty followed. When Mitch left for his and Cora's bedroom, Cora reminded Lynette and Anna to clean up. She then said that if the noise was kept down, the kids could stay up for a bit and watch TV. "Just remember to shut the thing off before you all go to bed, and don't stay up past ten. Oh, make sure you send Nina and

Joshua to bed by eight, they need more rest." With that she turned and headed off after Mitch.

As soon as the adults were in their beds, the games began. Although the TV was on, no one was watching. David and Caleb began wrestling on the floor, while little Joshua jumped from the couch onto them—giggling. Weee! He cried each time he made a leap. But after several successful jumps, Caleb tired of his sport and grabbed him. He then wrapped Joshua up into a ball and lay on top of him. Joshua cried for help, but no one came to his rescue. After he settled down, Caleb let him go. But by then the wrestling was no longer fun, so they decided to try something different, like pester the girls.

Anna and Lynette were in deep conversation with each other, and Nina was quietly sitting by their side listening. Her big blue eyes seemed to take in every word the two older girls were saying. It was then that Wendy and Christine took the opportunity to sneak outside and head for the horse barn. David and Caleb made several attempts to tease Lynette and Anna, but didn't get much of a rise out of them. In fact they were ignored to the point that the boys quickly tired of their sport and sat halfway quiet for a bit. Joshua grabbed a couch cushion, laid his head down and promptly fell asleep. With Nina's eyes drooping, Anna and Lynette carried the two youngsters to their beds still in conversation. Turning to David, Caleb asked, "How in the world can they talk so much?" Still a little put out that the older girls weren't more responsive of their attempts to pester them, David just said,

"They're girls aren't they!" Then he headed outside to look for Wendy and Christine with Caleb right behind him.

In the fort, the boys realized the girls had made some new improvements. "Come out come out wherever you are'" they mocked. But there was no reply. So they started looking through all the tunnels, yet they couldn't find the girls anywhere. "They're not here," said David. "Can you think where they might be?"

"Let's try the other barn, and if they are not there either, we'll try the hay field out back by the large oak cluster," replied Caleb. It was then that they heard the two girls giggling as they approached from outside. Wendy and Christine had seen the boy's skedaddling towards the big barn from the horse corral and quickly moved to join them. As much as they wanted to be with the horses, they dared not give themselves away—at least not yet. So soon they were all in the fort making more improvements. "If we make many more tunnels, there isn't going to be any space left for rooms," David uttered to no one in particular. Unaffected by the comment, the team kept building and before they knew it they were done.

"No more hay to stack without messing up a hidden tunnel or room," said Wendy and they all agreed that this was the ultimate fort.

Exhausted and still laughing, the team's satisfaction for their secret monstrosity was obvious. After diving though a couple more tunnels, Christine shared that they had better be getting back. "It's way past eleven and we do have to get up early," she said. With several disappointed sighs and moans the motley crew slowly headed back towards the house. On the way, Caleb whispered,

"By the way... what are the tuna cans for?"

"The what?... oh... for the lamps" Christine said. Without hesitation she continued, "As soon as we get come candles and matches, we'll have lamps."

"Wouldn't it be better if we just got a flashlight?" Caleb asked.

"Well, that would be OK, but a lamp has more mystery to it,"

Christine replied. "Besides, where are we going to find a flashlight that won't be missed?"

"Good thinking," He said. "And I do love mysteries! Ok, we'll get some matches if you get the candles."

Back at the house they found everyone else in bed, but the TV was still on. It was approaching the midnight hour, so they got a bit of milk to drink, turned off the boob tube, and turned in for the night. As the boys headed to their room, Wendy and Christine slipped down the hall to theirs. There would be six hours before breakfast and that was plenty of time for sleeping and dreaming.

CHAPTER 8

New Arrivals

So the routine started around the farm. Every day there was a long list of chores to do, and every night TV or games. Then every chance they got, Caleb, David, Wendy, and Christine slipped out for an excursion to the barn. Of course Wendy and Christine never let on about the "extra trips" they made to the horse barn. That is where the two girls were when the VW Bug pulled into the driveway Sunday afternoon.

Seeing the little car approaching from the corral, they quickly ducked out of the stalls and headed to the house to meet their mother. At breakfast, she had told them she was going to the auction to find a calf for Dagmar, and they wanted to see the new addition. When they got to the car, Betty was climbing out of the front seat and Cora was still in the back with a bundle of black, white, crème and red fur surrounding her. Betty opened the door and said smiling, "You can come out now—if you can, that is…" then she laughed.

"I can't move!" cried Cora. "The little buggers have buried me!"

"That's what you get for lifting your hand at the wrong time," Betty laughed even harder now. "I still don't know how in the world you all fit in there." It was then that Betty began pulling on the colored fur.

"You should have seen her…'" Betty said as the girls watched on. "She just couldn't keep her hand down! Every time a calf came into the ring by itself, she was a bidding! She must have spent ten dollars on those critters!"

"Oh, come now Betty," Cora's muffled cry called from the backseat. "You're going to love me in a couple of days when you no longer have to milk the cow!" "Besides, ten dollars is a heck of a deal for these calves!" Shocked surprise came across the two girls faces when they heard the word calves. And as they watched in total amazement, a black and white calf emerged. Then a crème colored one. Then a red and white one. And then another black and white one! Not one, not two, not three, but four calves stood bawling at them!

Betty said as she helped Cora from the back seat, "Girls, meet Hamburger, Scaloppini, Rapunzel, and Gretchen." Wendy and Christine's shocked surprise brought more laughter. As they stood there gawking, Christine couldn't help but notice there were two male calves and two female calves. "Mom?" she asked. "Are we raising the boy calves to eat and the girls to keep?"

"Well, since you brought it up, that is what we hope to do Christine" Cora replied. "Hence the names."

"Yippee! We're cowboys!" cried Joshua skipping down the front porch to see. All attention went from the calves to the little blond boy running towards them. "I'm going to be John Wayne!" More laughter erupted, and it wasn't long before Anna, Lynette, and Nina came out to see what was going on. "Wow!" "Would you look at that!" cried Lynette as her and Anna approached the crème colored calf. As she reached out to touch the little heifer calf she was greeted with a few small butts that brought more laughter from the crowd. And then Rapunzel started sucking on Anna's fingers. "That one is a Charolais, Gretchen and Hamburger here are Holsteins, and Scaloppini is a Hereford cross," said Betty. That brought several oohs and awes, plus a little respect from the onlookers as they tucked away this new bit of knowledge into their brains. This was going to be educational as well as entertaining.

Soon everyone was involved and helping to introduce the calves to their new mother. Although Dagmar didn't seem to mind, it was no small matter teaching the little guys where the faucets were for drinking. Finally, with full tummies the calves began to settle and explore their surroundings. They kicked up their heels, butted heads, and made soft mooing sounds while the children, Cora, and Betty escorted the menagerie towards the newly fenced back pasture that would now be the "herds" home. After a bit of fun with the new arrivals, the crew left the cow and her newly adopted babies to themselves.

That evening at the dinner table, there was plenty to talk about. There was a lot more laughter when Betty reiterated her story about Cora being stuck in the back seat of the little VW Bug with the four calves. "Well" Mitch said after the laughter subsided. "I hope that four calves are enough to keep us from having to milk that cow! Frankly, I would rather buy milk at the store rather than continue to take turns filling the bucket with aching hands."

"Now, you don't mean that..." Cora said. "She is a great

cow and with this crew our milk and butter bill would be atrocious!" "Besides" she continued, "Don't you like our homemade ice cream?"

"I do!" piped in Adrian. "In fact I could do with some right about now." With that, Betty jumped up and went after the ice cream maker while the kids all cried "Hoorah!"

Cora and Lynette went into the kitchen to mix the batter of sugar, eggs, and milk with heavy cream, while Mitch went after the rock salt and ice. With the batter placed into the ice cream maker now in the ice and rock salt, the hand crank began with Caleb applying muscle. Next came David's turn. Then the girls started. But before it got to Nina the ice cream was done. Adding a few fresh strawberries on top, Betty and Christine served the awaiting gang. While the families visited, each delicious bite was savored and some even went back for seconds. "Tomorrow we get to make butter!" Cora cried, and was amply rewarded with several "Oh No's and Oh My's."

When the ice cream was gone, Mitch commented that the fence would be finished the next day. "That means we can start fixing up the big barn for the tractor that I am buying next month. Then we will plant the hay field to new seed, and get the pond area dug." Adrian chimed in with "The hard work is starting to show. This place is really shaping up. I think we should get to that remodeling of the house, as winter comes before you know it."

"Yes, but if we don't get the fields and garden in, then we won't get a good enough crop to last us through the winter. So I agree with Mitch that we need to do the planting first, and then work on the buildings," said Betty. Adrian's disappointment was obvious, but he agreed that priority was the fields and garden. Trying to appease Adrian, Betty and Cora claimed the girls could handle the garden plowing and planting while the guys did the field and pond. "That will speed things up a bit" said Cora, so they could turn their attention to the building. Adrian was still brooding a bit, but quieted with the offer.

CHAPTER 9

Changes

WENDY AND CHRISTINE had made great progress with the gentling of the horses, and now could approach them without fear from either party. Although they had gained the horses trust, they still had not managed to climb aboard—nor had they told anyone what they were up too. Today would be different. Today, Wendy planned to ride Robin.

Having climbed up onto the hay feeder, Wendy waited for Robin to approach. When the red mare placed her head into the feeder, Wendy took the opportunity to quickly jump onto her back. Holding on for dear life, she clung to a gob of mane and wrapped her legs tightly around the horses belly as the red mare bolted for the door. At a full gallop, Robin passed through the corral gate and out into the field. She made a large circle with the other horses in hot pursuit trying to figure out what predator she was fleeing from.

Robin ran with reckless abandon and tried several times to dump the clinging thing attached to her back. She tried to duck out from under Wendy, tried to spin her off, and even tried to place her feet quickly in a new direction while running. But Wendy wouldn't let go. So in a panic, Robin made a run back towards the barn.

Seeing the small door just ahead, Wendy was afraid that Robin would hit the side and rub her off as she entered. So she called to Christine to step out and block the path. When Robin saw her way to safety had been compromised, she made a quick turn to dodge the corral gate and began another circle in the field at a dead run. This time Wendy had the mare's rhythm and could safely loosen her legs and glide with the movement. She began talking softly to the frightened horse, who responded by slowing her gait. Soon the two became as one and Robin gradually lost her fear. She slowed to a jog and rocked her ears as if listening to Wendy's soothing calls.

The commotion did not go unnoticed. Christine joined Cora, Betty, Lynette, Anna Joshua, and David as they approached the corral to watch. Although Cora was angry, she was also amazed at Wendy's obvious natural talent with the little mare. As the crew looked on, Wendy knew this would be her only chance to ride, so she prolonged it as long as possible. Wendy decided to try some new things. So she began putting pressure on the mare's sides with her legs. Responding to Wendy, Robin moved from side to side, turning as Wendy put pressure on first one side then the other. And before long the mare was totally at ease with Wendy aboard, following her every movement. When the little red mare finally tired, she returned to the corral with Wendy aboard. Sliding off gently as not to spook the mare, Wendy rubbed her head gently and thanked her for the best time of her life. Then she approached the crowd looking like the cat who ate the canary and ready for a scolding.

Christine looked at Wendy with admiration in her eyes, and the others were also in awe. Cora, however, was still a bit red-faced and her tone told Wendy she was not happy. "I guess it doesn't do me any good to tell you to stay off the horses," She said. "I'm sorry Mom, I just had to ride. Remember you telling me all the rides you took when you were young and all the training you did? I listened well Mom... I really did," Wendy replied.

"I can see that, but *I* did it with *permission*," Cora said sternly. Then softening a bit, "However, you do show some talent with the horses and you obviously have a strong love for them. So I am going to let you continue..."

"Yes!" Wendy and Christine cried together.

"Now wait a minute... I'm not finished..." Cora continued. "Only *with* supervision may you continue. I do not want you out here alone—ever! Do you understand?"

"Yes, Mom." "And furthermore I don't want you riding without telling me that you are doing so, so I can keep an eye out for you? Understand?"

"Yes, Mom."

"O.K. then. You may go ahead and ride Robin only with one of the others watching over you, and I will give you some instructions on training the others whenever I can get away. Promise me Wendy or you can forget about the horses!"

"Yes Mom. I promise." Wendy said a little too enthusiastically.

"Alright then. I'll expect you to keep me informed of your progress."

With a slight hesitation Cora and Betty turned back towards the house. "Do you think that is smart Cora?" asked Betty.

"Wendy will be OK Betty. Besides how else is she going to learn? How did we learn? It seems to me it was by trial and error and I think it is time to let the girls experiment a bit...only with some safety precautions in place."

"Well, it's your daughter—if she were mine, I would make her wait for me," Betty said as the two left earshot range.

"Wow that was awesome!" cried David. "I thought that mare was going to throw you for sure—but you showed her!"

"Yeah, and I thought she would wipe you out on the fence or smash you into the barn" chimed in Lynette.

"Aw! She didn't even buck or fall down. You're no John Wayne," said little Joshua disappointedly. Christine piped in,

"I knew you could do it Wendy! I am so proud of you! And now we can work the horses without having to hide it. I'm so excited! I can hardly wait for my turn..." The others just looked at Christine in amazement.

"What?" Christine said.

"You don't think I can ride like Wendy? Well, tell them Wendy!" Wendy shared that she thought Christine was a much better rider than her—at least she had a better seat in the saddle they had been practicing with. Then Wendy and Christine gave the other kids a tour of the barn and shared what they had been doing the past several months when they disappeared.

As the kids enjoyed the tour, the horses came into the barn to eat. So Wendy and Christine introduced them all to the horses one by one. Soon all were scratching necks and backs, feeding grain by hand, and enjoying the new four-legged friends. The horses had settled quite a bit since the two girls had been working with them and were definitely enjoying the attention now.

Playtime with the horses grew with the permission of the parents. Before long the riding skills of each of the youngsters were nurtured and they began bragging about how they could handle any horse, even if it meant a rodeo in the process. Some of the older kids were playing games on the horses like Knight and Armor where they knocked each other off with corn stalks, Cowboy and Indians where they threw pinecones at each other and if hit—fell off to simulate taking a bullet, or Dude Ranch where they played like idiots from the city—even climbing on the horses backwards! Some taught their horses to rear on command and others spent time learning dressage techniques and how to jump. As the talents grew, so did the challenges; however, summer was fast coming to an end and soon school would start up. Then the simple pleasures of the farm would change into more rigid schedules and less time for frolicking.

The hay fields had gone in smoothly and the garden was now producing. Huge crops of squash, tomatoes, potatoes, beans, peas, onions, lettuce, radishes, beets, peppers, and corn came from the garden daily. Fresh rhubarb, strawberries, raspberries, blueberries, cantaloupe, and watermelon graced the family's table and provided some income from locals in the community. In addition, several new plumb, peach, cherry, apple, and pear trees were planted and grow-ing around the garden area and yards. Plus a grape vineyard had been planted in the backyard patio area around a newly constructed and painted gazebo where a large picnic table now sat. A number of flowers had been planted in various places around the front and back yards and garden area to add color and provide sweet smells. Some of the flowers also helped keep certain pests away.

The large pond dug with the tractor and blade provided both irrigation and recreation. It was used to water the hay field as needed, and also supported bass, perch, and trout, as well as a couple of turtles. It also doubled as a great swimming pool where the family spent many nights of cool entertainment. The farmhouse was undergoing construction where the men were adding a new addition consisting of two bedrooms, a bathroom, and a small living room. They also planned to replace the entire roof and apply a fresh coat of paint before winter set in. All in all, the old place was totally transformed with the hard work of each family member.

One afternoon Cora went out to the old barn to review the condition of the old hay and see how much room was needed for the new hay due to come in the end of the month. She climbed on top of the large pile only to take a bad step and fall face first between ladder steps. She would have fallen on her head and may even have broken her neck if her feet had not been caught in the steps. She hung there for quite a while before someone heard her calling for help. Needless to say, once she was rescued, the fort was demolished and the kids all reprimanded. All the tunnels and rooms were removed, leaving only one large area with the top uncovered for sleeping and playing in. What a shame the boys thought…. It had been such a great fort with all it's secret passages. They would surely miss it.

The animals on the farm changed too. Dagmar, in spite of raising four calves, still produced enough milk for the two families until her calves were weaned. Then it was time to milk gallons again, so Cora went back to the auction for some more babies. Soon Athena, Beauty, and Freddie the Freeloader joined the herd. She also brought home eight bred ewes. The old sheep all had various problems, but Cora felt they could be cured and produce lambs. Caleb, Lynette, Anna, and Wendy learned how to doctor screwworms, maggots, and foot rot. Not to mention how to tag and trim the ewes in preparation for lambing.

After a couple of months of grain and alfalfa, Hamburger and Scaloppini grew to nearly twice their size and were ready to visit the butcher shop. A couple of weeks later they returned packaged for the freezer. Gretchen and Rapunzel were growing into beautiful young heifers while Dagmar was introduced to the neighbor's handsome Charolais bull. Next spring there would be even more baby calves and more milk.

Robin had her foal, a second buckskin whom Christine named Tiki. It didn't take long for Mike and Tiki to become fast friends—maybe they could tell they were brothers—who knows. As always, Wendy and Christine could be found in the barn playing with them whenever the chores were done. They loved just being with the horses even if all they did was clean in the barn and watch them frolic; however, they were riding Robin and Champagne when a huge yellow truck with wooden racks pulled into the driveway. Through the slats of the wooden racks, the girls could see several rough looking horses in the back. They scrambled from the backs of their horses, and quickly crossed the field to the driveway for a better look. Caleb and David were there first and when the driver asked for Cora, David went in search of her.

Emerging from the garden, Cora came to meet the driver. As she approached, he stepped out and shook her hand. "Thank you for delivering them for me," Cora said. "I wasn't sure how I was going to get them home."

"Anytime" the driver replied and he began unloading four of the horses from the group in the back. A dark buckskin mare Cora called Honey Bee who was very pregnant, a chestnut mare with a wide, white blaze named Gigolette, a bay mare named Gee Gee also very pregnant, and a solid chestnut mare named Pamahoe soon emerged and was led to the horse barn.

"Wow!" cried the girls.

"When are the mares due?" asked Wendy.

"Are any of them broke?" inquired Lynette who had recently joined them. Taking the multiple questions in stride, Cora answered them all. Although the mares looked huge, Honey Bee and Gee Gee were not due to foal until February sometime. Gogolette, and Gee Gee were well broke and available for the kids and guests to enjoy, while Honey Bee needed an experienced rider, and Pamahoe was,

"Totally off limits to all!" said Cora.

"Is she dangerous?" asked Christine.

"She is right now," said Cora. "But I am sure I can have her gentled down in no time." To which the driver smirked and then said, "I wish you luck lady! But that one should have been put down. She's plain crazy she is!" Then he climbed into the front seat of his truck and drove off with a wave of his hand.

Pamahoe was to be Cora's special project. As in her current state, she was indeed very dangerous. No one doubted she was completely crazy after watching Cora saddle the mare in the front yard and observing the wild thing explode straight up—snorting, jumping and bucking, then ripping the reins out of Grandma's hands, and finally bucking like a possessed thing until the saddle came flying off with a broken cinch strap. With blisters forming on her hands from holding on so tight until Cora could exit the saddle, Grandma wouldn't let Cora near the horse once she had let go. Mitch came running in from the field and quickly disappeared into the house. When he reappeared a few minutes later with a rifle in his hands, Cora stopped him at the door. "Please Mitch... I can tame her. I know I can." "Cora, this is nuts! She really *is* dangerous and you know our rule about that." "Please..." said Cora again. "She will be a big help on the farm with the cattle. Besides I really like her—she reminds me of when I first met you…a diamond in the rough?"

Then Cora smiled at him. "I don't know. I am really worried about this one and am inclined to agree with the driver that maybe she should have been put down a long time ago." Yet Mitch slowly put the rifle down. Cora immediately went out to retrieve the saddle off the ground and return the mare to the corral. After that, everyone but Cora keep their distance from Pamahoe.

CHAPTER 10

WITH GREAT ABUNDANCE came great expectations. Soon members of the Church were coming out to the farm for barbeques and horseback rides. The family also hosted several missionaries in route to their next mission field. Neighbors joined in on the activities and birthdays were celebrated, holidays enjoyed, and monthly game nights established. The work seemed to never stop, but neither did the fun. The farm was a healthy way of life and definitely good for the heart and soul.

The horses had become such a big part of the girl's lives; they were all given a horse for their birthdays. Lynette got Gigolette, Honey Bee was given to Anna, Robin became Wendy's, and her foal Tiki, was to be Christine's—although Christine would ride Champagne until Tiki was old enough. Betty claimed Gee Gee and Cora had Champagne and Pamahoe. The foals to be born from

Honey Bee and Gee Gee were also to be Cora's, since it was she who purchased them all to begin with. As for Nina, well she wasn't quite old enough to have a horse of her own, so she would have to wait a couple of more years.

Whenever they could, the girls rode in the nearby hills enjoying the pleasures of having four-legged friends. The boys didn't seem to care that much for the horses, but occasionally took a ride with the ladies or used the horses to herd up the growing cattle herd. Cora made progress with Pamahoe and was riding her daily now. Although still cautious as the beautiful mare tended to spook, she was learning and settling down. Also true to her word, Cora taught the young girls how to ground break a horse so that it was ready to ride before you even climbed up on its back. She and Betty started up a 4-H club and taught proper care of horses, their anatomy, common illnesses, and a fair amount about breeding. They also got the girls involved in participating in local parades and horse shows.

Before they knew it, it was time to harvest the hay fields and put the new crop into the barn for winter. Mitch was on the tractor making bales, while Adrian and Caleb were collecting the bales for transport to the barn. Wendy was in the back yard with Anna and Betty helping to harvest the last of the garden squash when someone yelled "Fire!"

Mitch jumped off the tractor, grabbed a hose and ran for the smoking hay barn. Everyone else ran with buckets and shovels. "Hurry! Over here!" yelled Caleb.

"We need water here now!" cried Betty. Wendy dipped her bucket in the pond and passed it down a line that had formed with Christine, Anna, Grandma, Lynette, Cora, and Betty. As fast as they could they sent buckets of water to the fire and back trying to douse the flames. David was running back and forth with a bucket too, as was Adrian and Caleb, while Joshua and Nina looked on helplessly. Adrian hollered "Over here Mitch! Quick it's getting out of hand!" Mitch was spraying with the hose, but try as they might to stop the flames, it was too late and the crew had to back away from the heat of the now raging fire.

As they helplessly watched the large barn go up in smoke, the crew sat in silence. When it was over, they surveyed the scene before them. The grand old structure now lay in a pile of ashes and charred wood. There was no trace of the hay and other materials that was once inside. Only dirt, ash, a few nails, and some wire lay in the piles of still burning coals. "Well…at least we didn't get the new crop of hay in before it burned," said Cora.

"Yeah, and there weren't any animals inside," piped up Christine.

With a sigh and slumped shoulders, Mitch replied sarcastically, "That's keeping a positive attitude."

Betty quickly asked, "Is everyone all right?" Several haggard yeas and uh-huhs followed. The tired crew made their way slowly back to the house still finding it hard to believe the big barn was gone.

Later that evening, each of the kids were questioned as to what had happened. After all the stories were told, all were lined up for a spanking. Only Joshua escaped the punishment, as the parents had thought he had been too little to participate in the hay fort and its surroundings. Even though Christine and David were the ones who had actually lit the candles, all the rest of the youngsters had been involved in trying to light matches for the tuna can lamps. Christine and David had just been the first to succeed. Once lit, Christine had placed a candle under a floorboard in the barn while she and David ran to get the rest of the gang. The old dry hay had immediately caught fire and it didn't take long for the flames to build into a full-blown fire engulfing the large old wooden structure. That is when Adrian had spotted it and yelled for help.

The loss had been significant to the family. It would be a long time before they could build a new structure to replace the one lost and that would mean the hay would suffer in the winter weather. Not to mention the loss of shelter for the cattle and sheep. The horses might even get a little rain rot if they weren't careful—and what would the little babies do? Wendy would always remember the lesson learned that day and would never again play with matches. Nor would she allow anyone else to.

CHAPTER 11

GRANDMA AND GRANDPA
went back to Medford shortly after the fire. School had started back
up and time with the horses got shorter. Even so, Christine, Anna,
Lynette and Wendy spent many a day riding on the surrounding
hillsides. They had found and named several special places—wol-
verine cave, bone hill, ghost hollow, pee-wee creek, and lone rock,
to name a few. Each of these places had its own story to tell and
each trip into the mountains brought a new adventure.

Once Wendy had Robin fall on top of her on an old logging
road when she slipped in the mud while her and Christine were
chasing a deer. Luckily when the two went down in the mud and
Robin's hind leg caught Wendy under the arm then shoved her out
from underneath her belly with flailing legs. As soon as Wendy
got to her feet, the mare was able to get up. Wendy removed the

mud from her eyes just as Robin realized she was free. The mare bolted for home. Wendy yelled as loud as she could for Christine, who had missed the incident and was still somewhere ahead on the trail. It was then that she realized just how muddy she was. There was not a dry spot on her, and her entire head of hair was a great big mud ball. But there was no time to worry about it now, and when Christine came back looking for her, she jumped on behind double so they could beat a trail back to the house before anyone worried.

A riderless horse always brought trouble…as, it normally meant that something had gone wrong and someone was hurt. So if a rider did not make it home with their horse, the adults would immediately come looking for them in a panic. When the rider was found, the situation for losing the horse would be thoroughly considered. If the adults determined the loss of the horse was unavoidable, then the rider would be allowed to continue their horse excursions within a few days. Yet if the adults decided that the rider had been irresponsible, they lost riding privileges for quite some time.

But somehow Christine and Wendy managed to enter the driveway hot on the heels of Robin. Which was a good thing, because their mother had spotted the loose horse running down the road towards the house and was already on her way out the door. Her worried look turned to a grin when she saw Wendy. And she couldn't stop laughing. Cora had never seen a human mud ball before!

Then there was the time they ran into a rusty barbed wire fence blocking their newly found deer trail. Christine got the bright idea to lay a coat over top of the fence so the horses could see the top wire. After jumping her horse over without a hitch, the other girls took turns jumping over the wire fence before collecting their coats and continuing the ride. It was to be a method they would use often when traveling great distances where fences seemed to have blocked them inside. It not only saved a long ride around the obstacle looking for a gate, or the cutting of wire—which a lot of riders chose to do. The girls, however, had a reputation of not damaging things, which gave them favored status with neighbors so they could ride pretty much wherever they wanted. No one stopped to think of what would happen if one of the horses missed...they simply knew their horses would make the jumps.

The crew also got to where they would look for trees that bent towards the ground in kind of an arch. They called these trees "Hawaiian walkers," as they could climb them with ease to see what was off in the distance. They would normally build a fort of some kind around these trees with corrals for the horses and shelters for sleeping under. Although they didn't really spend very many nights up on the mountainsides, they always had a place to go if they wanted to. They were building one of these forts when they heard a couple of rifle shots and a bullet came streaking past them! They had forgotten it was hunting season, and without a rider, the buckskins looked like wild game to some. You never saw girls move so fast, as they grabbed their horses yelling as loud as they could, mounted, and ran for home! From then on, much to the girl's disappointment, riding was completely off limits during deer season.

Then there was the time when someone stepped in a yellow jackets nest while riding through thick trees. As the horses ran away bucking from the stinging bees, the girls dodged branches and tree trunks while desperately trying to get the yellow monsters out of their hair and clothes! Big welts soon showed up on several places over the horses hides, as well as on the girls arms, legs, necks, and backs, making it clear that no one escaped without at least a couple of war wounds. From then on the crew was very respectful of beehives in trees and well as in the ground and kept a keen look-out for any sign of the miserable creatures.

Swimming parties normally put the fun back into a "challenging day." In the river, the riders took turns taking their horses into the deep water for a roller coaster ride out. They would strip to their underclothes and swim with the horses for hours. Christine's horse loved to dive, so they found themselves stacking—from the neck to the tail—on it's back while waiting for the horse to jump off the edge into the deep water. Some would fall off during the ride, while others held on throughout the entire swim. Splashing, laughter, and sheer excitement always followed. When everyone had enough, they would lay out on the banks soaking up the sun's rays while the horses grazed peacefully nearby. Sometimes they would scout about for new treasures or additional spots to add to their collection of special places. Many picnics were enjoyed along the banks of the river and several forts were built in secret places. It was always so much fun; the girls could hardly wait for the next ride.

However, it wasn't long before the Tendicks had to leave for California for a short time. According to Cora, they would be gone at least a month wrapping up the last ties of their old place in Shingle Springs. Yet when they returned they would be free to build a new home in Oregon. Cora and Mitch had promised them five acres of land on the farm to build a home on, and they went to make the necessary financial arrangements. With the Tendicks away, the girls would have to pick up a few extra chores, leaving them very little time for the horses and riding. Oh well, Wendy thought... at least it would only be for a month.

She was daydreaming about what she would do when the

Tendicks returned and they could all finally get back to riding. But when she got off the bus, she knew immediately something was terribly wrong. A strange car was in the driveway and they were greeted by the neighbor lady Maxine, whom Wendy had not seen since they had first arrived. As she scanned the front yard, Wendy asked in a rather shaky voice "Where's Mom? What's going on? Why are you here?" Flustered, the large woman said,

"Now don't you worry none honey, your Momma is going to be all right. Just gather a few of your things, as you will be staying with me for a few days." Gasping, Wendy said,

"What do you mean Mom will be all right? What's happened?" Not waiting for an answer, Wendy ran for the house with Christine, and Lynette close on her heels.

"Mom? Mom! Dad!" Wendy yelled. But no answer and a quick scan of the inside told her no one was there…the house was empty. Turning back towards Maxine, Wendy repeated her question "What do you mean Mom will be all right?" Three sets of wide eyes were now on Maxine who did her best to calm them and get them packing.

"Like I said honey, you need to gather a few things. You three will be staying with me for a little bit until your Momma comes home from the hospital. Now don't you worry any…she has broken her hip and will have to stay there for a bit." The girls were not to worry. They were to pretend they were on holiday for a few days and everything would work out just fine.

According to Maxine, their mother had taken a fall from a horse and had been found in the ditch beside the road by a neighbor driving by. The neighbor—Brenda she thought—had called an ambulance which had taken their mother to the hospital. Cora had broken her right arm and left hip. She would be fine and coming home soon, according to Maxine. The large woman further shared that she had volunteered to help out with the girls since their father had already left for California to help the Tendicks family with some problems they were encountering. They were still trying to get a hold of him to let him know about their mother's misfortune and share that everything was under control. And even though the girl's grandmother was coming back up to help out—it would take her a few days to get things together and get here.

Hurriedly Wendy ran to her room for some clothes. Christine and Lynette quickly joined her and all started talking at once. "Broke her hip! Oh my…I hope she can walk!" "I wonder if it hurts?" "When do you think grandma will get here? Do you think she will stay long?" "Took a fall from a horse…you don't suppose she was riding Pamahoe alone do you?" When Maxine entered to see how they were doing, the girls were packed and ready to go with her.

The first few days went by quickly and the girls did have a bit of fun. Maxine and Walt, her husband, were like grandparents to them. The older couple spoiled the girls rotten—giving them ice cream, candy, and just about anything the girls showed an interest in. Lynette was having the time of her life, as Walt and Maxine were very wealthy. When Lynette noticed a baby grand piano in their front room, she offered to play it for them. The Taylors were so delighted with her performance; they asked her to play regularly thereafter. So each day the crew enjoyed a musical concert where Lynette's fingers flew over the keys and she sang to her hearts content.

All three girls tried hard to please and help out, as to not be too much of a burden on the couple; however, with each passing day, the girls began to really miss their family and got more and more worried about the animals. Wendy asked if they could stop by and check on the horses, but Maxine told them everything was being taken care of. Walt, sensing the emotional state of the young girl, invited her and Christine to join him at the barn to take care of his prize Charolais bull. The beast had caught a cold and Walt was giving him shots of penicillin. He assured the girls that he could not handle the bull alone and they were delighted to help.

Yet when the few days turned into two weeks, Christine and Wendy got more than restless. "I'm sorry Maxine, I don't mean to sound unappreciative" started Wendy, "but it has been two weeks since we left the farm and I am really worried about our animals. We have a couple of mares that are coming due to foal soon and I would really like to see my mare Robin."

"Yeah, and I would like to see Tiki too" said Christine as she plopped herself down into a nearby chair. Looking into the girl's anxious faces, Maxine finally spoke.

"Well…I guess I could talk to your father about it this evening. He is home now taking care of things…They moved your momma from the hospital to the farm last Wednesday, and your Dad asked for a little bit of time alone with her. He is probably ready for you girls to come home and get back into the routine again too." Maxine's hesitant posture made the girls wonder if there was more she wanted to say, but she didn't continue. She just sighed and left the room. The girls were so excited they nearly burst! Mother was home from the hospital and they were going home to see her! They practically skipped as they went to find Lynette to give her the good news.

But Lynette wasn't at all happy with their glad tidings. Although she was glad to hear their mother was doing fine, she had grown accustomed to being spoiled and rather liked how she was living at the moment. She didn't want to return home to the chores and family just yet. Besides, here she had her very own room…maybe she could ask if she could live with the Taylors for a while longer…

Early the next morning the girls each gave Walt a big hug before climbing into Maxine's car for the trip home. They were going to miss him, but could also hardly wait to get back. When they pulled into the driveway they barely let the car stop before opening the doors and springing onto the front porch. "Mom! Dad! We're home!" Wendy cried. Christine ran right behind Wendy and they bolted into the living room at the same time. There they skidded to a stop. In the corner was a large hospital bed that held Cora. She was hooked up to all kinds of pulleys and strings. Her right arm was in a cast and she was bruised on the forehead, cheek, and collarbone. She smiled at them and told them to come give her a big kiss.

Maxine and Lynette came into the room with Grandma Mary right behind them. "Sorry Cora, but the girls wanted to come home." Maxine shared.

"That's alright Maxine. Mitch and I can't thank you enough for helping us out. We really do appreciate all you and Walt have done for us."

"Let me know if there is anything else you need," Maxine replied. Then she turned and left, talking briefly with Grandma Mary as she exited the room.

Afraid that they might hurt her, the girls gently and carefully went forward to give their mother a kiss on the cheek. "Don't worry" said Cora. I won't break. Plus I will be out of this contraption and chasing you girls around in no time." She smiled at them reassuringly.

"Don't you believe it!" Grandma Mary said as she reentered the room after having walked Maxine to the front door. "The doctors are saying she might not ever walk again! But until she is healed up and we know more, you girls are going to have to pick up the chores and stay out of the way. Understand? Now go get ready for school, you have been out way too long!" She hustled them out of the living room and into their bedrooms.

Wendy got dressed in a hurry and skipping breakfast, ran outside to make a quick trip to the barn before the bus came. She was nearly to the barn when she realized something was wrong. She entered the barn only to discover Robin, Tiki, Gigolette and the two Tendicks horses, Honey Bee and Gee Gee. Pamahoe, Mike, and Champagne were missing. So she ran over to the hay field for a look. There was nothing...no horses, no sheep, no cows, no calves. Nothing. So she made a quick trip around the front and back yards and pastures. Still, Wendy found not a single animal besides the few horses when the bus pulled into view.

She was out of breath when she reached the bus and climbed aboard. "You almost missed it," said Christine.

"I wish I had," Wendy replied as the bus pulled away. "All the animals are gone...except our three horses and the Tendicks' mares."

"What do you mean?" Christine said in shock.

"They're gone! I said..." Wendy snapped back at her.

"Well excuse me!" said Christine. I didn't mean to ruffle your sensibilities! I was only concerned." And with that Christine changed seats. Guilt at treating her best friend roughly quickly overtook concern for the animals and Wendy turned around to face Christine. "I'm sorry. I shouldn't have yelled at you. It's not your fault, I am just really worried. Forgive me." But it was too late.

If they changed seats now, Mrs. McKinzie would send them home with a note, as no one was allowed to be up or change seats when the bus was moving or they were immediately suspended. And they had all ready missed enough school as it was. It was going to be rough catching back up with their classes and her grades had not been that strong anyway. Besides, Wendy needed to collect her thoughts. Still, she wished Christine were sitting with her so they could put their heads together for some planning. This was all too much with mother in traction and the animals missing… dad conveniently nowhere to be found, and the Tendicks still in California.

CHAPTER 12

California Plans

WENDY MANAGED TO KEEP
her wits about her over the next few weeks. Although it was not
easy with Grandma Mary who constantly kept them busy and who
ushered her and Christine out of the house every time they tried to
talk to their mom. To the girls, it felt like Grandma was trying to
keep things secret—away from them anyway. Possibly information
they would not like or approve of. This made the girls very jumpy
and apprehensive. Not to mention a little resentful.

Other than the three horses, the animals were indeed missing
from the farm and there had been no explanation as to where they
might be, who was taking care of them, or when they would return.
Also, their father seemed to always be gone when they got home.
In fact, they had not talked with him since they had returned from
the Taylor's. So Lynette finally asked where he was, Grandma just

said he was in California somewhere helping the Tendicks. Her body language told them she didn't approve of his absence and the most they learned from her was that with the rush trip home to be with mother after the accident, Mitch had left unfinished business waiting for him and the Tendicks back in California. According to Grandma, he had left several days ago to go take care of them. When Lynette asked if she could go back and stay with the Taylors until he returned, Grandma just gave her more chores to do. After that no one asked her any more questions.

Trying to stay out of the way, Christine and Wendy went back to riding as much as possible. Grandma always found them in or around the barn when she did come looking for them and that is where she found them now. "Girls…your mother is due to come out of traction today, and your Dad hasn't made it home as promised. Although I can remove the traction gear, she will need to go to the hospital to have her castings removed. I am going to have to take her myself, and I need you, Wendy, to take care of things here. It will take us most of the day and may even go into the evening. So I need to be able to count on you. Can I?" she asked. "Of course," replied Wendy. Christine and I are used to watching over much more than the horses Grandma. Is there anything else you need for us to do?" "Good" she said. "And no I don't need you to do anything else. Just keep an eye on things. Your mother and I will be back as soon as we can." Turning with a sigh, she left the barn.

The girls were glad for a reason to stay home from school. Yet, with all that was going on at home, it was hard to keep their grades up and Wendy was worried about her upcoming report card. Although she liked her classes, she just couldn't concentrate. "Christine, how are you doing in your classes?"

"Oh, I'm doing ok. I think I am getting a B in history and a B in science. But I am pretty sure I am getting A's in all the rest. How about you?" Hesitating a bit, Wendy slowly shared her concerns.

"Well…to be honest…I am a little worried. I have been trying, but I can't seem to get into the lessons right now. Just too much going on at once I guess…"

"Maybe we should spend some extra time in the books tonight," Christine commented. Wendy shook her head in agreement.

"Thanks for your understanding and support little buddy." To which Christine responded with a grin from ear to ear.

The girls finished up feeding and straightening the barn area, and then went to the house to get breakfast and hit the schoolbooks. They hadn't been at it for very long when Mitch arrived home. When he entered the house, he was in rumpled clothes, unshaven, and looked very, very tired. "I drove all night, but bad weather held me up in the Cascades. Where is your Mom?" "Grandma drove her to the hospital a couple of hours ago," said Christine. "And Lynette is in school. We got to stay home, as Grandma wanted us to keep an eye on things." Wendy just nodded in agreement. Looking from one to the other, Mitch smiled and said

"Good." "Because I have been waiting for a chance to talk with you two anyway." He then wrapped his arms around the girls and gave them a hug.

"I am sure you have noticed a few changes around here since the accident." When they both nodded their heads, he continued. "I am sorry, but I had no choice but to let the animals go. I just couldn't take care of them and your mother at the same time, and with the Tendicks family gone, I couldn't find help on such a short notice. Not for that many animals anyway.… But at least I was able to hang onto your horses for you." Shocked at what their father told them, they tried hard to not let their feelings show. Both girls told him they appreciated his efforts at keeping their horses safe. Then they both said at once,

"You really let *all* the other animals go? What did mom say?"

"I did what I had to do, with or without your mothers blessing, as I had no choice!" He said heatedly. Wendy nearly broke into tears, but managed to say sheepishly

"Wow Dad! We didn't realize things were that tough…" When Mitch realized her face had turned red and her eyes began to water, he continued more softly but still very firmly.

"Look, I am very sorry, but as I said there were few choices for me with everything that was going on. My hands were full with your mother and I didn't know what else to do."

"That's ok Dad. We understand." The girls repeated together as numbness began to creep over them. With a big lump in her throat Christine tried to think of something positive…anything…. She saved the day by switching the subject to their recent stay with Waldo and Maxine.

"We had fun at the Taylors' Dad! They were real nice to us. We helped Waldo with his sick bull and also helped feed his cattle herd." That was all Wendy needed to stay the tears and collect herself. She was once again grateful for her little sister's quick thinking and support.

"I'm glad to hear that," Mitch replied. "Anyway… there is much more to be done. With all the medical bills we have incurred, we could lose the farm. Even with the sales of the hay and livestock, I don't have enough to cover the bills and still provide a decent living for you all. So I have accepted a job back in California. I will be returning this weekend and sending for you two, Lynette, and your Mom the first of the month. The Tendicks will be moving into the farmhouse to take care of everything here until we can return. I'm not sure how long it will take, but we will come back and live on the farm again down the road sometime." Surprised by all that their father shared openly now, the girls did their best to take it in stride. Although, they were happy to finally know what was going on, the news was far worse than they had imagined. For now they would do their best to be supportive and keep a stiff upper lip. Later they would deal with having to leave their four-legged friends behind.

After sharing the news with the girls, Mitch knew he had to get some rest. Excusing himself, he went into the bedroom and sat on the edge of the bed. Mitch was pleased with himself. Even though he had sold the animals more from anger at Cora, than from not being able to find help to care for them, he knew he had done the right thing. Besides, now the stupid animals won't tie them down anymore and he and his little family could get back to the things in life that really mattered. Back to the city where he could make a good income and continue growing his career. He really liked being the top salesman on the west coast and all the benefits that went along with it—and he was sure the girls would get over their infatuation with the animals in no time—look at Lynette…she knew the value of the city life and the joys it brings. Maybe her talent in singing could be exploited as well…oh yes, the possibilities were endless…

Anyway, he just wasn't ready to go back to farm life like Cora was. He had too much of it growing up with his eight brothers and sisters when his Dad had died and he had to take care of his mom, the younger kids, and the farm. Then he had enlisted in the army so Cora would marry him, and well…it was more than he had bargained for. Now he just wanted Cora, the girls, and maybe a son to carry on the family name. Oh yes, and the good life…he was more than ready for some of the good life that only money could bring. As he thought about it, he realized he was tired of being a hypocrite...going to church, attending Bible classes, playing host to people who wanted to see the farm—when all he wanted was to take Cora away and enjoy life a little. Why put yourself through all that? Right now he decided he needed a little "me" spoiling. And with Cora in the condition she was in, she wouldn't have much to say about it. She would just have to deal with what ever he decided was best for them, and in time she would come to agree with him. Satisfied with himself, he lay back on the bed and was soon snoring away.

Returning to their studies, Wendy and Christine couldn't help but think about the forthcoming move. They were getting depressed at the thought of leaving and sat in silence for quite a while pretending to read. Finally, Wendy broke the silence. "I wonder what it's going to be like. I'm guessing it won't be much different than when we left. Remember? There were really big schools packed with kids who weren't very nice. Some even offered us drugs and others kept bugging you about wanting to make out...never mind that you gave up your morals or worse...might get pregnant. It was all in fun they said...And if you didn't go along with them, you became their mortal enemies and they did everything they could to be mean to you. I remember how they used to throw basketballs at my head in PE when the teacher wasn't looking. Or taking my gym clothes and putting them in the toilet. But the worst was their running into you on purpose in the hallways trying to knock you down. I really got tired of all that crap!"

"Yeah," said Christine. "They were not at all like this little country school, where all the teachers are friendly and actually cared about your success. Where there were no locks on the lockers, and you still sang God Bless America."

"Or that the kids expect their parents to do everything for them, and are more interested in money and having a good time, than they are about each other," Wendy interjected. "And all the people! I remember clearly that in California everywhere we went there were great crowds of rude and unfriendly people." Wendy's memories of shopping with people running to and fro and inevitably running into her with their shopping cart still gave her the willies. They would just give her a look of "get out of my way!" They wouldn't dream of giving her an apology for running over her in the first place. And the high crime rate…all those robberies, rapes and murders! With most going unreported. It was really scary. "I sure hope we will all be safe in our new home."

"Me too," said Christine. "Do you think we will be able to fit in even a little?" "This last year has made me realize just how much we have changed. I feel so lucky to have escaped all that ugliness we left behind. Mom was right to insist on us coming up to Oregon and living out in the country…even though it has been hard work, it has been worth it—big time!"

Wendy began to worry anew, "I certainly hope we don't go right back into what we left. I really don't think I could take it again. I guess I am just not meant to be a city girl…"

"Me neither," Christine replied taking a deep breath and letting it out with a loud sigh. It became pretty clear that they would no longer be able to concentrate on their homework. So rather that sit and stew, the girls opted for their favorite pastime…a ride. Closing their books and taking a last minute check of the house, out to the barn they went.

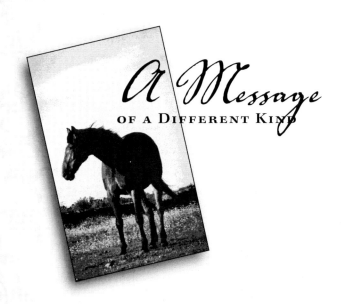

CHAPTER 13

A Message
OF A DIFFERENT KIND

BOY IT FELT GOOD TO BE on the back of a horse Wendy thought as she rode. The horses and girls had just climbed to the top of Hunt Gulch, when they spotted something white moving in the distance about half way up the next hill. "Wonder what that is!" exclaimed Christine cantering up to where Wendy and Robin were.

"I don't know…but let's get a better look." With that the two girls raced their horses down the jeep trail towards the white object. As they got closer, it began to move. "I think it's a…I think it's a goat!" cried Christine.

"Are you sure? What would a goat be doing way up here?" Wendy was skeptical.

"I have no idea why it would be up here, but I am positive it is a goat," replied Christine.

As they got closer they could see that the white object was indeed a goat. An Angora goat to be precise and it had long wool that was all entangled by a dead tree snag. The goat tried several times to free itself, but it was caught fast. So when the girls came to a halt, Christine dismounted and handed her reins to Wendy. Approaching slowly and carefully, she climbed onto the old wooden log to where the animal was caught. It took several minutes, but she was able to loosen the wool from the snag and free the frightened animal. Once freed, the goat ran a short distance and stopped. It then turned around and cried 'baah'—as if to thank her. Then it came forward and cried a few more times before turning and disappearing into the underbrush. "Well, that is a sight you don't see everyday," Wendy was saying. "I think it was trying to Thank you Christine. Or maybe it wanted to go home with you! Ha!"

"Who do you think it belongs to?"

"I haven't a clue. Maybe we should ask around. It is no doubt lost and the owners are probably really worried. I know I would be."

So the girls remounted and headed back down the trail. They made a wide sweep of the area looking for possible homes where the goat may have lived. After stopping at four homes in a ten-mile radius and having all the homeowners deny having ever owned or even seeing a white goat, the girls decided the animal had been a special omen sent special to them. They reasoned the goat was sent for the specific purpose of reassuring them they would be "unstuck" or "freed" from their own troubles soon. At least they hoped it was so.

Besides, they *had* heard adults talk of a great spiritual being who lived in the Heavens and sent messengers or 'Angels' to earth.

These angels were tasked with watching over people to keep them safe from harm and to provide messages on an "as needed" basis. So Wendy and Christine decided that maybe this was their 'Angel' of sorts… Anyway, what ever it was, dark was fast approaching and the girls had to get home. Besides, Wendy didn't want Grandma to think she had not done her job of keeping an eye on things. Treasuring the moment in their hearts, the girls turned their horses towards home and raced for the barn.

When they entered the house a little bit later, Grandma and Cora were already back. Cora was sitting in a dining room chair beside Mitch, who almost looked like he had been crying. At least his face was red. And Grandma was busying herself around the living room where she could keep an eye on things from a distance." Lorraine must be in the bedroom where the music was coming from, thought Christine. It was then she noticed the wheel chair next to the table and let out a small gasp, drawing Wendy's attention to it as well. Cora looked up and spotted the girls.

"Good. You're back. We were just discussing your Dad's new job and our upcoming move."

"Yeah, that was before I learned that your mother here is confined to a wheel chair" Mitch said.

"Mitch, I told you, it will only be for a short while. I will be up and walking around in no time. You'll see…and it won't stop me from doing my—" He cut her off.

"I knew I should never have let you keep that crazy horse!" He said angrily as he stood to his feet. "And now our choices are very limited!" He then excused himself and headed for the bedroom before Cora had a chance to say anything more. Besides, things were really going the way he wanted them to, so why push it. Cora now had no choice but to follow him back to California—like it or not.

Catching her breath, Cora said "Don't mind him girls. He is just a bit upset right now. He is worried about the Doctor's news, but what do they know anyway…" "Now come give me a hug!" Wendy and Christine ran and gave their mother a hug like never before. "Wow!" said Cora. "I guess you did miss me!" The girls smiled back and asked what they could do to help.

"Yeah, what do the doctors know" mumbled Grandma under her breath sarcastically. Cora gave her a look of, come on mom; I need your support right now not your negativity. To which Grandma responded by leaving the room to go find something else to do to keep her from worrying.

Cora continued her conversation with Christine and Wendy. "Well, right now we need to think about moving. According to your Dad, we will have a truck arrive next week to pick up our things. Then we will fly down to Sacramento where he will meet us and take us to our new apartment." A noise from the corner drew their attention to Lynette sitting in an overstuffed chair across the room. She was smiling from ear to ear. So she wasn't in her room after all, Wendy thought. She was surprised at Lynette's display of enthusiasm, but realized that her older sister could hardly wait for the trip to start. Lynette always did like the finer things in life, as she had made that pretty clear when they stayed with the Taylor's. But Christine and she were from a different mold it seemed, and this move was going to be tough on them. Especially since their horses wouldn't be coming with them. Yet it was important that they keep their attitudes positive for mother's sake.

"Mom… What will happen to our horses while we are gone?" asked Christine. "No one will sell them will they?" Wendy and

Christine tried not to show anxious faces as they gazed at their mother.

"Over my dead body!" said Cora. "I know how much those horses mean to you two. And selling them is NOT an option. The Tendicks will be back shortly—maybe even before we leave—and they will watch over them for us until we either return or send for them. I have already talked with Betty about them and she told me no problem on their end." Both girls breathed a heavy sigh of relief at this news. "Now, since the horses will be staying for now, there is no need to pack the barn stuff. So, Wendy, in the morning you will begin boxing the kitchen and bathroom. Lynette, you will be responsible for the laundry, pantry, and living room. Christine you will help me with the bedrooms. And Mom, can I count on you to help pack odds and ends and clean?"

"Of course you can dear," replied Grandma from the kitchen. "I am here for what ever you need me for." "Thanks Mom," Cora said with a smile and a wink to the girls.

CHAPTER 14

Moving

WHEN THE TRUCK PULLED
into the driveway a few days later, everything was packed and the
crew dressed comfortably for a long trip. The loading didn't take
long, as there really wasn't much going. Everything being moved
fit nicely into boxes and what little furniture there was, stayed for
the Tendicks, along with all the garden, barn, and farm equipment.
Grandma Mary had been a big help, even though she grumped a
lot. She must have had a hard time watching Cora struggle, because
she hovered over her like a little baby. Soon the positive attitudes
of the girls won her over and as she drove them to the airport, she
cried. "See girls. She is not as tough as she thinks she is. Life has
just worn her down," Cora said as they all waved goodbye from the
sidewalk.

The plane ride flew by and when they landed, Mitch was

there to pick them up. "There you are…Wheelchair and all! Are you ready for a surprise?" Even though he was teasing them, he was anxious to get going. In no time, he had gathered their bags and wheeled Cora from the baggage area to the awaiting car. Once everyone was in their place, he started the car and cried "Off we go!" Boy he was in good spirits Wendy thought.

It didn't take long to drive from the airport to the town of Fair Oaks, and within minutes they were pulling onto Orange Avenue; however, instead of an apartment complex, they pulled down a long gravel driveway. A very nice older home on a little over an acre of land greeted them. "I thought you would be more comfortable out of the main part of the city," Mitch told his family. "Besides, we may be able to have a horse or two here for you girls, when I can afford to ship them down." That brought yells of joy and glee from the backseat. "And I have a surprise for you too Lynette," He said looking into the rearview mirror at the older redhead. As the car came to a stop, Mitch climbed out and retrieved the bags from the trunk. The girls responded by promptly vacating the vehicle.

At first quick glance, a beautiful manicured green lawn surrounded by huge shade trees and bright colored shrubbery came into view. A light brown and ivory brick walkway lined with several ornate trees guided their pathway up to the front door. There, a very large cement fountain, cascading water from a sirens water bowl spilled into a basin below. Upon closer inspection Wendy could see that the basin, or pond, was filled with of lilies, rocks, water grass, and a variety of goldfish. Several large green plants of various shapes and sizes, she wasn't sure what kind they were, surrounded the fountain and filled the plant beds on both sides of the entryway leading to the front door. As they entered the house, the family found a variety of new furniture scattered about. "Where did you get all this?" Cora said incredulously as she began looking around the kitchen they had just entered.

"Well, it so happens, that it came with the job," Mitch replied smiling broadly. "Right out of some of the fancy mobile homes I am selling—" He was interrupted by a scream that came from the front room.

Wendy and Christine darted around the corner to see what had caused the commotion, only to discover Lynette standing mouth agape in the middle of the room staring at a large brown upright piano. When Lynette collected herself, she went over and lovingly ran her hands over the beautiful instrument. Then she sat down and starting playing. "Oh father! Thank you! Thank you!" she kept saying as her fingers flew over the black and white keys. Poking his head into the room, Mitch shared,

"There is also a small barn and garden area out back" then he winked at the two younger girls. Wendy and Christine didn't need any further encouragement, and quickly raced for the front door.

Although Cora wasn't entirely convinced of Mitch's explanation of how and why things were the way they appeared, she let it go for now. "Well, you are full of surprises aren't you?" was all she said. Mitch smiled and relaxed for the first time in weeks. He was sure Cora would come around to his way of thinking, but for right now it was just good to have his little family all to himself again. Yes, there were some changes they would still need to work through in the days yet ahead, but right now it was time to get comfortable.

Later in the week when the truck arrived to deliver the boxes, the family was pretty much settled in. Lynette had her very own room and was quite delighted with her newly treasured piano. She had decorated her space with large posters of her favorite singers and had placed musical instrument trinkets throughout the bedroom. She also had an array of photos of famous places she had hoped to visit someday strung about. There was Paris, Rome, London, and Madrid—Singapore, Beijing, and Tokyo. The Bahamas, Tahiti, Australia, and New Zealand, as well as, Puerto Vallarta, the Amazon Rain Forrest, and the Congo graced her walls. When you stepped into her room—if you got beyond the mess—it was quite an education in 'worldly life.' Although Wendy thought it might be interesting and fun to see all those places, she didn't really care for the décor. But Lynette and her friends went wild over it.

As usual, Christine had 'buddied up' with Wendy to share a room. Only this time they shared a large queen size bed instead of the normal bunk beds. Also as usual, they had filled their room with horses and riding paraphernalia. Various materials made up the display of different breeds and colors of miniature horses that now lined their dresser tops and shelves. In addition, a wooden barn that the girls had made from scraps of wood found in the barn, sat in the corner. A couple of plants hung from the ceiling and several more adorned the plant stand by the window. A trophy case awaited their ribbons and trophies still yet to be unboxed, and a used western saddle sat on a rack next to the bed.

Besides their room, Wendy and Christine shared space in the barn. They had fixed up a spot for their tack, feed, and other horse supplies. They had encountered several black widow spiders and mice while cleaning out a grooming area and fixing a stall. So in anticipation of the horses arrival, they got their Dad to spray pesticide inside and out, plus lay out a few mousetraps. Also to help out with the mice problem, Christine brought home two cream colored kittens she planned to raise in the barn. She announced that these tiny creatures would keep the mice from taking over.

However, the kittens were so cute, the girls had a really hard time leaving them in the barn. They often snuck them into their bedroom for some special attention, sometimes letting them sleep at the foot of their bed before hurrying them out in the morning before the parents got up and got going. They named the short-haired one Tabitha and the longhaired one Cream Puff. What fun the fuzzy little creatures were! And the girls just knew they would be good mousers because they sure did attack their prey—ribbons, strings, and even fingers—with the greatest of ease and yet as fierce as lions! They would have trouble keeping them out of the mouse-traps though…so those would have to go.

Cora was given a special room where she could comfortably sit and oil paint to her hearts desire. The room had several windows that let the light in and gave her a view of the neighborhood. She had three sizes of easels, a desk filled with stacks of paint tubes, brushes, sponges, and other painting supplies, a small table, and two very cozy chairs. She also had a small projector that she used to shoot slides up on the wall so she could get a good outline for larger pictures. When Cora wasn't painting, she would go to the garden in the backyard and mosey, or just sit in the patio area. Although she tried, in the wheel chair she didn't have many options.

When he was home, Mitch could usually be found in his small shop where he loved to build things, or with mother barbequing in the backyard. He was the best cook ever, Wendy thought…boy could he ever make chicken and steak taste good! Her mouth watered just thinking about it. Besides everyone having their own space, the property had lots of trees and a small pond on it. So it didn't feel like you were in the city at all. Everyone was comfort-able in a very short period, although Lynette—Wendy was con-vinced—would have chosen to be much closer to the city lights.

CHAPTER 15

Time flies

THE NEW SCHOOL WASN'T nearly as bad as Wendy and Christine had imagined, although it did have a certain roughness about it. There was a crowd that wore all black and smoked at the outside edges of the building and sometimes ridiculed or picked on other students. There was a lot of talk about drugs and guns, but Wendy never saw any of them and both she and Christine did their best to stay away from the "darker side" of things. So, for the most part, school was a lot of fun and offered many opportunities for the girls.

Wendy loved her teacher…he was a Jewish man, whom she learned more than just the basics from. Math, science, history, and English were only part of the lessons Mr. Mashado shared with his class. He also taught practical things like how to build a wooden chair, making candles and soap, and photography, to name just a few. Mr. Mashado introduced his class to a variety of different cultures through dancing, art projects, and guest speakers. He expected the kids to perform at their best and encouraged them in every situation. His high standards and positive support got the respect of even hard core kids, getting unexpected performance from them and in some cases, changed lives. Needless to say, Wendy was sure Mr. Mashado was the best teacher ever!

Christine thought her teacher was equally great and the two girls often discussed the pros and cons of their educational environment. They also participated in some of the after school programs such as track and field, tag football, and drill team. In addition, Christine ran for school counsel, so Wendy was kept busy being a campaign manager and helping her get elected. Whew! They worked hard to stay busy so they wouldn't have much time to miss their four-legged friends.

They also did their best to stay in shape. When weather allowed, the girls would walk to the school facilities a little more than three miles away from their house. They really enjoyed walking, as the streets were lined with lots of fruit trees that they could help themselves to along the way. Wendy especially liked the pomegranates while Christine loved the cherries the best. Sometimes Lynette would walk with them and her favorite were the nectarines. She also never tired of discussing all the cute boys in all her classes. Although the two younger girls would listen politely, they really weren't interested in the boys. They did however enjoy their older sister, as she could really get them laughing with her stories. But Lynette's walks were rare, as she preferred her new friends to her sisters.

Wendy didn't really mind Lynette's absence because Lynette and she had very little in common anyway. Besides, with Christine as her best buddy, she didn't need anyone else; however, Lynette's continual discussions about all her new friends did prompt Wendy and Christine to go meet their neighbors. And after introducing themselves, the girls found their neighbors to be very friendly. It wasn't long before they had several new friends regularly joining them in playing games in the back yard. 'Kill the Carrier' and 'Sheep and Wolf" were the favorites played by an ever growing group. The youngsters even got several of the adults to play along with them every now and then. Then when they weren't playing games, they went frog hunting down by the pond.

Cora even got into the swing of things by having guests over for morning coffee or dinner on a regular basis. She also got into the habit of inviting visiting missionaries over to spend the night to share their adventure stories with the family. Although she had many friends and enjoyed them all, she seemed to really have a good time with Bev from across the street. Bev had a daughter named Lynn, who quickly became fast friends with Lynette. The two older girls dreamed of making it big in the music world, taking exotic travel tours, and dating rich men! Christine and Wendy thought they were nuts, and began wishing even more that their horses would soon arrive.

Yet as time went by, it seemed that Mitch had forgotten about his promise to bring the horses down from Oregon. Wendy and Christine were getting increasingly apprehensive, but didn't get the chance to talk with their father about the problem, as his job kept him so busy they rarely saw him. However, as the frustrations grew with their father, their inspirations grew because of their mother. Cora was not only making great progress in getting rid of her wheel chair and walking in spite of what the Doctors had said, she was a great supporter of the girl's loves and dreams. Even though she knew she would never ride again, she felt she owed it to her daughters to help them be able to enjoy their furry treasures. Besides, Cora had determined herself to live life through her girls, and one day she shared with Christine and Wendy that she hoped to be able to ride with them again. Knowing that their mother could hardly walk, let alone ride, the girls really appreciated her enthusiasm and quietly listened to her share old stories and plans for the future. They in return would tell their mother their hearts desires and favorite riding stories. All hoped that someday their many dreams would indeed come true.

Time flew by and Wendy couldn't remember all the things that she and Christine did together. As usual they kept themselves busy so they would not miss their horses in Oregon so much. Their father had still not sent for them, nor even mentioned them, and the girls were beginning to wonder why. Could it be that once again there was something being hidden from their soft hearts…? Wendy couldn't help but speculate.

When Christine and Wendy learned from her mother that immediately after the accident their father had sold all the animals more from anger than from not being able to find someone to help with them, they lost a fair amount of trust in him. Especially since he had told them differently just a few days before they packed for their trip down south.

According to their mother, Mitch had been furious when he found out that Cora had been hurt and may never walk again— and in retaliation—sold everything. That is everything except for the girl's three horses… and even then he didn't really want to keep them… saying he felt strongly that horses were dangerous animals not to be trusted. The only thing that kept him from selling the girl's horses was mother's threat to leave him if he did.

Learning of their mothers fight to help them keep the loves of their lives, Christine and Wendy tried hard not to burden her with constant questions about the horses. Lynette didn't seem to care much about hers, but for Christine and Wendy it was very difficult to be patient; however, when they really got concerned, one of them would ask their mother if there was any news. She would normally reply that the horses were doing fine and she was working on their father to get them brought down. Cora would say, "You'll just have to be patient a little bit longer girls. Your father is just being difficult about them for some reason that I just don't understand. Probably because of the accident, he is afraid that you will get hurt too. I must say I worry a little more than I used to, but I also know that you two are great little riders who take every precaution to be safe. So I will continue to work on him until we get them for you." Then she would hobble off to go do something in the kitchen. Even though it was slow going and often hurt her in the process, she refused to use her cane. She just couldn't bare the thought of being a "cripple" as she put it.

Mitch seemed to be gone all the time now, rarely making it home for dinner. The only reason the girls knew he was around was because of the dirty clothes and dishes he left behind. Even the weekends found very little time with their father; however, one morning Wendy got up to find him in the kitchen taking his time before leaving for work. He had just poured himself a fresh cup of coffee and reached into the silverware drawer to fetch himself a spoon to stir the cream. When Mitch pulled his hand out of the drawer, he came out with a brown racer coiled around his hand. He jumped back shrieking and shaking his hand to remove the critter tightly fastened to his arm and Wendy honestly thought he was going to have a heart attack! So she grabbed his arm and removed the snake.

Cora chose that moment to enter the kitchen. When she realized just what was happening, she couldn't help but burst into laughter…which didn't help Mitch's mood any. That is when Wendy informed him that she had lost her pet snake earlier in the week and couldn't find it anywhere. She had thought the snake had been lost forever and thanked him for finding it. After recovering from the freight, Mitch made Wendy get rid of her entire snake collection. Never again was she allowed to bring a snake, or any other reptile, into the house.

Wendy secretly thought it was justice for having lied to them about their horses. But she never told him so. As for mother, she was wonderful! They enjoyed several trips to the American river for picnics, parades and rodeos, school plays and concerts, and neighborhood functions. Cora always volunteered her time to help out, even if she was still a little slow at getting around. Her face always had a smile on it and folks sought her out because of her encouragement.

Cora's paintings were also growing in number and beauty. In fact, Wendy couldn't remember having seen such wonderful wildlife scenes before. Her work was wonderful, and she even sold a couple of paintings to the local bank. One of a stagecoach scene, and one of the Sacramento River with a herd of deer grazing along its banks. Wendy felt the Elk picture was her best, but the bank wanted a local touch for their customers to enjoy. Wendy was so inspired, that she even tried her hand at painting. But even with her mother's help, she didn't seem to be very good at it. She did however, have a lot of fun trying and thought that maybe one day she might actually be able to paint something worthwhile…with a little more practice of course.

Her two sisters were a little bit better than she at the artistic side of things. Yet, along with the entertainment came several trials by her siblings. Especially with her older sister Lynette, who constantly did everything she could to ignore her chores. She had grown very lazy and was getting messier by the day, and Wendy often had to pick up after her. And whenever Lynette wanted to get out of doing dishes, she would go to the piano and practice. Cora loved the music so much she would allow Lynette to wiggle out of doing her part, which made the other two girls a bit resentful at their older sister. Especially, when she began to abuse the privilege, sighting the days were just too full to get everything in—school work, practice, and chores—even when both Wendy and Christine knew she spent hours talking to her friends on the phone. So when Wendy came in from the barn one Saturday morning and found Lynette on her bed instead of her own, she was really angry at her sister. Wendy shook Lynette awake and told her to get out of her room and go to her own room. When Lynette sleepily replied there wasn't any room on her bed, Wendy stormed out and opened the door to Lynette's room. There she discovered a heaping mound of clothes on Lynette's bed and things strewn all over the floor. She was so mad at her sister; she went back into her own room and promptly shoved Lynette off her bed onto the floor. She yelled at her sister, telling her that if she was going to live like a pig, then she could sleep like one too! That was when Cora intervened and broke up the fight, sending the two of them to their own rooms until they could be civil to one another. To which Wendy thought would be a mighty long time if it were up to her!

Christine on the other hand, had become "miss goodie two

shoes." This was the real reason for Wendy's irritation as of late. She was miserable when Christine would act so sweet and innocent around mom, saying how wonderful everything and everyone was—including their older sister—when all along Wendy knew she felt differently. Christine would share her true feelings of frustration with Wendy, but then would say nothing but positive things around their parents. This created a slight drift between the two, and Wendy didn't know what to do about it. Although she agreed that they should try to be positive, she also felt that they needed to address their concerns and problems. Christine also seemed to be getting interested in a neighborhood boy who lived a couple of houses away and whom she spent a great deal of time catching frogs with. Wendy was beginning to feel really lonesome. And without her best friends—the horses—to turn to, she was getting desperate.

Yet time seems to heal all wounds and Wendy soon found herself getting more involved in school. Her dedication to her studies was beginning to pay off and she was getting A's and B's in all her classes. When she decided to try out for track, she discovered that although she was an average runner, she was an above average high jumper. Soon she was on the team, and after a couple of meets, she broke the school record with a five-foot four inch clearance. That was quite a jump for a five-foot girl, making her the star of the team! Boy did that feel good!

But stardom was short lived, as the lead girl of a group of freshman began shoving her around. At first Wendy was polite—saying she was sorry and excusing herself; however, this only encouraged the girl and whenever one of her gang members was present, she would intentionally knock Wendy's small frame around. Finally, Wendy got tired of the bullying and hauled off and slugged the girl in the stomach—demanding that she apologize. When the girl fell to the floor trying to catch her breath, she began to cry. Wendy told her to never touch her again. She returned to her group with a whole new appreciation for Wendy's strength. I guess being a farm girl did have its advantages. The gang never bothered her again.

As time passed Wendy began to see that she was changing. Her heart struggled with a longing for her horses and her best friend seemed to have left her for other company. Although she and Christine still did things together, it just wasn't like old times. Wendy really missed those old times and often dreamed about more adventures.

CHAPTER 16

Return to the Farm

DAYS TURNED INTO WEEKS
and before Wendy knew it, three years had slipped by. She had gotten so wrapped up in her dreams and school; she had nearly forgotten the farm in Oregon. All except the horses, that is. Those she
never stopped thinking about. Yet when the family pulled into the
driveway, the flood of memories came rushing back. She now had
mixed feelings about returning—as the last time she had seen the
place the family had been leaving her favorite four legged friends
behind amongst a pile of troubles.

Her heart still ached for Robin and her stable mates, as her
father had not brought them to Sacramento as he had promised.
Even though there had been a place for them, he seemed to never get
around to making the arrangements. Cora, however, had purchased

a couple more horses that had kept them busy as of recent and were now in the four-horse trailer being pulled along behind them.

Things had changed quite a bit since they had left. Now the Tendicks lived in the old farmhouse, which they had extensively remodeled once again and the Newmans' were to build the new home in the back of the property. Besides purchasing the house from Mitch, Adrian had built a new barn where the old big barn had burnt to the ground. It was a single story and it kept all the hay from the field dry, plus provided a covering for the animals that the Tendicks now owned. The horse barn that Wendy and Christine had so carefully watched over had been turned into quarters for the cattle, and all the horses had been turned out into the large hay field.

The yards and garden area had really grown up. The fruit trees were now producing fairly large crops and the garden supplied more than ample food for both families. The Tendicks not only sold produce to others in the community, but also donated extra food to the church. Adrian had joined the choir and the family had regular attendees from the church over for barbeques and farm fun. It seems that they always had someone visiting…

There were also a couple of new additions to the Tendicks family—goats! And it didn't take long to learn the goats were escape artists. Therefore they had free rein of the porch, front and back yards, and even the front room! The few leaves still left that hung within reach of a stretched lip ambling up from unsteady hind legs showed evidence of this fact. Not to mention the little pebbles of poop they left for everyone to step in on your way up the steps and into the house. Mitch was not too happy with the goats in the home, but then again, it was no longer his house to worry about.

When Wendy made it out to check on the horses, she found

Robin to be pretty much the same as when she had left. The little red mare came right up to her for a scratch, and she swished her long red tail in warning as the other horses came up to see that the new visitors were and to see if there were any treats to be had. Wendy could tell Robin was as spunky as ever and could hardly wait to get back up on her back. But that would have to wait for a bit, as they had not yet settled in.

Robin's colt, Tiki, had grown into a very nice boy. His buckskin color had darkened and his muscular body was powerful, yet sleek. Betty had shared that she had him gelded since stallion issues made the family nervous with all the little children that came and went from the farm. Betty also shared that Tiki really needed some training, as he seemed to have a bit of a stubborn streak in him. Wendy thought if he was anything like his mother, Christine would have her hands full. Even so, Wendy knew it wouldn't be long before Christine would be running over the hills with him.

Gigolette too had darkened in color. She was the same sweet thing she always was and she was a favorite of guests who came to the farm to ride. The little herd had grown with the Tendicks' mares both foaling shortly after the Newmans' move to California. Honey Bee had a palomino colt they called Tequila and Gee Gee had a dun colored filly named Taffy. Both were three now and both were in need of breaking. Then when Cora added her new four—Queen Patron, Bandoleer Prince, Tonka, and Melody—to the growing band, the field was full of color and talent.

Bandoleer Prince, or "Bandy" as he was nicknamed, was a young quarter horse colt with a very promising future. Queen Patron was his mother and they were the only two purebreds on the place. Queen had a racing background with two very talented parents, both who were high money earners on the racetrack.

Queen had won over fifty thousand dollars herself, before sustaining and injury to her hind leg and being retired to broodmare status. Bandy's sire was also a top money earner, making him an excellent choice for a future breeding stallion for the farm; however, right now he was too young to realize that he was a stallion and with his very gentle nature, was allowed to run with the girls in the open pasture. Melody and Tonka were mostly quarter horse with a bit of thoroughbred mixed in. Tonka was black and Melody chestnut. Both were nice riding animals who enjoyed the mountain trails. Cora had bought them for packing into the backcountry, something Wendy had not yet done and was very much looking forward to.

It wasn't long before the family settled in and the girls were riding all over the hills again. Although things had changed a bunch, Wendy was back in her element and never felt better.

CHAPTER 17

Building
A NEW PLACE

IT DIDN'T TAKE LONG before Mitch fenced off twenty acres and set up a camp trailer for the family to live in while they built their new house. Building began and within a few short weeks, the frame was up and the entire home plumbed and wired. The bathrooms were completed and a couple of bedrooms sheet rocked to provide some privacy so the family could move in. Living in a house that you are building is full of challenges and definitely takes its toll on the nerves; however, it didn't take long for the girls to discover that after being sent to bed, they could sneak into the rafters and creep down into the living room area to watch a favorite television show or two. If mother looked up and spotted them, they could be back in bed with the covers pulled over their heads before she could get down the hall to their rooms. Even though Cora was pretty sure the girls faked sleep, she rarely scolded them, and it became a game to see how long the girls could go before being discovered and having to flee to their bed for the night.

Once the entire place was sheet rocked, taped and textured, the little game they had invented ended. Then with the Tendicks and Grandma Mary's help, the roof was completed, the siding put up, and finishing touches done both inside and out. Shortly following the building of the house, there came a new garage, a barn, and a corral. Then they put a swimming pool in the back behind the new garage. Once the landscaping was completed, Wendy was sure they had created something really special. Christine also felt an incredible awe for all that had been accomplished and the two often talked about all the things they were going to do on this new "mini ranch."

As soon as the family settled into the new place, new animals came to the farm. And the creativity never stopped, especially when it came to the games. Wendy and Christine played John Wayne—named for Joshua—where they jumped off the barn roof onto the backs of unsuspecting animals, then ran around the corral whooping and hollering, laughing and singing! They built tiny model ranches in the dirt, much like you would use a sand pile for playing with trucks. They used items they found in the surrounding area for their masterpieces. For example, they used pieces of bark for house material, small pine cones and little grass clumps for trees and bushes, sticks for fences and pens, and Christine even found some clear plastic that she used for a swimming pool. They made roadways to their places, and placed little plastic farm animals in the pens. These building projects provided many days of entertainment.

However, one of the girls' favorite games was to sneak out their bedroom window when everyone was in bed and go for a moonlight ride. They would wait until they could hear Mitch snoring and then they would creep out the window and out to the barn. They would each grab a hackamore and catch a horse. They would then carefully open the corral and lead their mounts out the driveway and down the road a ways before climbing aboard. Then off they would go talking dreamily and riding into the early morning hours. Finally, the girls would return as stealthily as they had left.

One night, Wendy suggested they include Anna and Nina on their midnight excursion. So before catching their horses, they snuck down across the field. Tapping on the girls' window, they waited for it to open. Anna and Nina arranged to meet them on the hill at peewee creek. Nearly twenty minutes later the crew were enjoying the moonlight and telling ghost stories. What fun they had! Even though it was dark, they trusted their horses along the trail and knew they would get them home safely.

It was then that Nina heard a rustle in the bushes. "What was that!" she said stopping her horse suddenly catching the other girl's attention. Then they all heard it. The bushes not six feet away were moving and rustling loudly, bringing their mounts to full attention. As the girl's hearts raced and they looked around for an escape route, they heard snickering. Wendy let out the breath she was holding and said in a strong voice "Ok boys! You went and scared us good! So you can come out now."

Caleb and David came out of the bushes laughing. "We heard you talking in the moonlight outside the girl's window planning a night get away. So we decided on a little fun of our own," David offered. "We are Snipe hunting…" piped up Caleb.

"Snipe hunting? What is that?" the girls asked in unison.

"Well, its when you take a gunny sack like this one, and drag it behind you like so, then you hit the ground in front with a stick. In the dark, the snipe get so confused they run right into the bag, thinking it's a safe place."

Now it was the girl's turn to laugh. "You mean that you actually believe that this 'snipe' thing is going to run into the sack you're dragging behind you when you hit the ground with a stick?" said Christine.

"How stupid do you think we are!" cried Wendy. "Nothing wild is going to run towards trouble, no matter how confused they are. The animal will either stay put hiding, or they are going to high tail it as far away from you as possible!"

"That's not true!" Caleb defended his game. "I happen to have it on good authority—from Uncle Butch himself—that the snipe do in fact run into the bag when they are scared!" He had stopped laughing and was rather irritated at Wendy for questioning this supposed knowledge. Undaunted, he and David turned to begin their snipe hunting excursion. Whistling and hitting the ground, they walked down the jeep trail in front of them. "Well, enjoy!" hollered Anna over her shoulder as the four girls took off down the hill still chuckling.

"Boy, and I thought I was gullible," said Christine.

"Yes, but don't worry, we will get our chance to get caught doing something really silly soon enough," Wendy replied.

"At least the boys aren't doing anything dangerous or mean," Nina piped up.

"That's true,'" said Anna. Then the girls continued their chatting as they into rode off in the dark. They discussed everything from silly games to more important things like the new building plans for grandma's home. From relationships of their friends to the 4-H horse club Betty and Cora were thinking about heading up. But as usual, the conversation always ended up in a discussion on how each of the girls longed to raise a barn full of colored horses and all the talent they would have in their barn. Adventures were always at the top of the list, with the raising of foals next in line.

Wendy secretly hoped to have a foal of her own in the near future. In fact, she had given a lot of thought to this recently, as she had seen Bandy mount her mare Robin a couple of months ago. At first she thought he was just playing, but then she noticed his manhood was out and he was actually breeding her. Wendy had never witnessed a horse breeding before and was quite amazed at the beauty and grace of it all. The young colt had strutted around the mare like a peacock, sucking up his belly and arching his neck. Nickering gently and teasing her with little nips down her side until she stood for him. She had casually mentioned this to her mother a few days later, who responded by immediately having Bandy removed from the field and put into a pen of his own. She told Wendy that she was pretty sure that he was too young for her mare to conceive, but that it was possible that she would have a foal. Of course Wendy hoped for the latter.

Such the talk and thoughts went as the girls rode into the night. In fact, they had so much fun, the time went by a little too quickly and they barely got their horses back into the barn and into their beds before the sun started coming up. It was a good thing that it was Saturday so they could sleep in just a little bit.

CHAPTER 18

The Healing

THERE HAD BEEN MANY such excursions into the night over the next several months and the girls became a very close nit group. Even Lynette joined them from time to time for a jaunt onto the hillside. Their secret rides in the night were their favorites as they always ran into something new when they went.

Then one morning when Lynette, Wendy, and Christine meandered into the kitchen for breakfast, both Cora and Mitch were there waiting for them. The girls were surprised to see their father as he was normally already gone to work when they got up for school. However, this morning Mitch was not only present, but he was smiling from ear to ear!

Then the girls noticed…their mother was singing and moving around the kitchen like nobody's business—in fact, she was even sort of skipping and running! "Whoa! What happened!" cried Christine with Wendy chiming in right behind her. "Mom! You're running…when could you run?" Lynette was just as excited "And bending! You couldn't do that before—what is going on???" the three girls could hardly contain themselves as their mom and dad's smiles turned into joyous laughter.

Cora quickly explained that she and Mitch had been invited to a church meeting in Medford the night before. Since it was such a long way to go, they had nearly passed on the invitation until Aunt Betty called and told them she and Adrian would meet them there. Betty had also shared that Aunt Cindy and Grandma Mary also wanted to join them, as they had heard that the speaker was a highly thought of man of the Christian faith who had been rumored to have had people in his services healed from various problems. They were all very curious and wanted to learn more. Even Great Grandma Elizabeth was to be there.

So Cora and Mitch had driven the three hundred plus miles to Medford where they met the rest of the family before being seated in a Church pew about six rows back from the pulpit. They listened quietly as the Pastor shared how his life had been changed when he met Jesus Christ, God's son, whom he had invited into his life to be his personal savior. He shared that just because he had been raised in the Church, and his father was a minister, it did not automatically make him a Christian. He shared that unless you have a personal relationship with God's only son, Jesus Christ, you are not saved and ensured of going to heaven when you die.

Then he began to share his personal testimony about how he came to know and love Christ. He shared that in college he had rebelled against his parent's faith and got into alcohol, drugs, and women. What started out as a good time, before long completely took over and nearly destroyed his life. He dropped out of college, lost his part-time job, and was so depressed that one night he decided to end his life. Just as he raised the gun to his head, a knock sounded at his door. Hiding the gun between the cushions of the couch, he went to the door and opened it.

There he found a young Christian man with a Bible in his hand. He asked the Pastor if he knew who Jesus Christ was. When he didn't answer, this young Christian began to share the scriptures—the books of John, Acts, and Romans—and how Jesus had changed his life personally. Something clicked inside the mind and heart of the Pastor. Although he had heard it many times before, this time it got through and the tears began to run down his face. The Pastor learned for real that we are all born sinners, are destined to die and go to hell, yet are loved by Jesus Christ so much, that he died in our place so that we could choose to be with Him in heaven when we pass from this world. So teary eyed the Pastor asked Jesus for forgiveness and invited him to be his personal savior—to come into his life and change him. From that moment forward the Pastor had been serving in the mission fields and Church, witnessing many people's lives changed by Jesus.

Cora could relate to this Pastor's story, as she too had been raised in a Christian home. But she had never invited Christ into her life as her personal savior thinking that she was saved by going to Church and being a good person. Something tugged at her heart and told her everything the pastor had said was true, so she bowed her head on the spot and invited Christ into her life.

While she was praying, the Pastor introduced a guest speaker from Corvallis, Oregon. His name was Jim Galligan, and he was a "faith healer." When Mr. Galligan took the stage, he gave his own testimony of being saved by Christ, and having the Holy Spirit tell him he would become a "healer of the people" for Jesus. Not really understanding the significance of what had been spoken into his heart, he nearly forgot about it. Then he had been at a farm where a young child, around four years old got bucked off a horse and badly broke his leg. As the child screamed and struggled in pain, Jim and the boy's father ran over to him. The leg was clearly broken in more than one place, and without thinking, Jim placed his hands on the broken part and began to pray in Jesus' name. The child immediately quit crying. When Jim dared to open his eyes, the leg was completely normal. Jim was so shocked he just stood there as the boy got up and got back on the horse. If Jim and the boy's father had not both witnessed it, they would never have believed the leg had been broken.

"That was how Mr. Galligan got started in his ministry," Mitch piped in. He then went on to share how Mr. Galligan began to pray for two women at the meeting. The first woman had headaches that started at the back of her head and wrapped around to the front. They were so severe the lady could not function normally and was forced to sit in pain for hours. As Mr. Galligan went into more detail about the injury, he prayed that Jesus would heal this woman. Next he prayed for a lady who had a hip problem. It was her left hip and it interfered with her ability to walk, bend, squat and other normal movements. Again he went into more detail and prayed in Jesus' name for this lady to be healed. While he prayed, Cora felt a heat come over her body. And when he was finished praying and she opened her eyes, all her family were staring at her!

Cora said, "That was me. He was praying for me!" Mitch informed her that it was impossible. Unless someone who knew her had requested prayer, it could not possibly be her that Mr. Galligan prayed for. But Cora kept insisting that it was she. She also said that all the pain she had been living with since the accident had left from her body and was completely gone! None of the family had made any kind of request for prayer, and Cora didn't know anyone else there. The family, who had been at the meeting, had a hard time understanding what had just happened since none of them had ever witnessed a miracle before. It was much easier to assume Cora had just thought it was her that had been prayed for.

So after the service, Mitch went up to Mr. Galligan and asked him who the ladies were that he prayed for. Jim shared that he did not know their names, and only the Holy Spirit had told him to pray for two women, so he did. He further told Mitch that the woman with the headaches had just come forward and shared that she felt she was healed as her headache had disappeared as he prayed. Mitch then hesitantly said that he thought his wife might be the woman with the hip problem. After further clarification with Mr. Galligan, Mitch was finally convinced that Cora was indeed the one prayed for. Had his wife really been healed as she claimed?

Yet the fact that she could now walk, bend, squat, and run as she was currently showing her two sisters and mother, was all the proof that was needed. The family was so excited they could hardly stand it! They had much to discuss after the meeting so Mitch and Cora had been delayed and only arrived home a few minutes before the girls came down for breakfast.

Wendy was the first to ask what it means to invite Jesus into your life. So Cora explained that inviting Jesus into you life means that you believe Jesus was the son of God, that He died in your place for your wrong behaviors and actions which we call sins, and that you invite Him to come into your life and change you. Once you do this, you become a child of God. Then when you die and leave this world behind, you go to heaven to meet the Lord Jesus. Yet while you complete your life down here, you must work to show that your life is really changed by being obedient to His word—meaning reading your Bible, acting on the guidelines it gives you, praying and spending time with God, and doing your best to love and serve God by loving and serving others. She further explained that over time God tests you to see how you're progressing. This is done by allowing problems to come into your life that you must learn how to handle. Eventually you learn skills, knowledge, and patience that mold you into a mature Christian, who can then help others learn how they too can change their life through a personal relationship with Jesus Christ.

All three girls wanted to know more, and over the next several weeks they had many discussions with their mother. When Wendy understood the sacrifice that Jesus had made for her and her family, she knew what she had to do. Alone in her bedroom she got down on her knees and prayed. "Dear Jesus. Thank you so much for taking my place on the cross. I am so sorry for all the bad things I have done. Please forgive me. My temper is bad, I say things I shouldn't and do things that I know I am not supposed to do. Forgive me…please please forgive me…" The tears ran freely down her face as she continued. "Jesus, I believe you are the only Son of God. And I know that you love me and my family and all of my friends more than I could even imagine. So I am asking you to please come into my life and change me into the person you want me to be. I want to make you smile. For I love you too. In your name, Amen." When Wendy got up off her knees a great weight had been lifted off her shoulders. She felt like dancing! She immediately ran to tell Christine what she had done.

Over the next few days both Christine and Lynette also

accepted Jesus as their personal savior. Cora and Mitch heard back that as a result of Cora's healing, several other family members and friends gave their lives to Christ as well. Still others, who had drifted from the Christian faith, renewed their relationships. And suddenly, life took on a whole new purpose…as the entire family—aunts, uncles, cousins, sisters, brothers, and grandparents—began displaying major changes in their attitudes, behaviors, and actions.

CHAPTER 19

More Adjustments

AS EACH FAMILY MEMBER made changes in themselves, they also made changes to the landscape around them. Soon Grandma Mary was building her new home on a five-acre plot with support from the entire family. Each member contributed where they could and the framing, roofing, and finish work were completed in record time. Grandma's new home was very unique, as she had made a grand entry with a huge rock fireplace acting as a separation wall from the living room and a formal dining area. Every rock in the floor entry and fireplace came from rocks she had collected over the years as she traveled throughout the United States. She also included rocks given to her by other family members and selected at least one rock found by each of her nine grandchildren. Her many treasures were embedded into the beautiful masterpieces including crystal, obsidian, turquoise, petrified wood, agate, and several other precious stones. Each treasure had a special memory attached. Her love for the beautiful rocks was contagious and soon several of the grand children—including Wendy—had a new love for rock hounding.

Wendy loved the rocks so much; she began to collect her own pile of treasures for a future fireplace of her own. Once when she was out riding with Christine down by the creek, she discovered a splash of orange in the bank. When she dug it out, she had discovered the largest agate she had ever seen! Carefully mounting and placing the large stone on the withers of her mare, she rode straight to Grandma's with her new found treasure. Grandma confirmed it was indeed an agate and she asked if she could take it to her rock club. It wasn't long before they learned that this particular agate was the largest found in the entire region and Grandma won a special award for showing it at the fair.

As rock piles began to grow in Grandma's yard, Aunt Cindy and Uncle Jim McClusky decided to move up from California and build a new home too. They selected the five acres between the Newmans' place and Grandma Mary's to put their new place on. Yet before they started building, they got an opportunity to purchase a much larger farm about four miles down the road. It took just a few days for them to decide to go with the older farm already built instead of erecting a new one.

When they moved in with their daughter Cathee, things got very busy. Now there was more remodeling to be done on their farm, as well as the Tendicks. In addition, Grandma's yard wasn't done yet, and neither were the fences between the five-acre lots separating the new homes. As family members stretched their time and resources to the max, they withdrew from regular visits and most entertainment.

Maybe it was just her imagination, but Wendy couldn't help but wonder if there was more going on than seemed. As winter settled in, everyone was just too busy to ride, and the morning coffee visits had nearly stopped. Wendy had discussed the pulling back of family relationships with Christine earlier, but she hadn't had any insights either. Wendy would just have to talk to their mother about it the next time she got the chance. But for now, she needed to get her chores done and think about what she was going to do for Lynette's upcoming sixteenth birthday. Sixteenth birthday's are supposed to be special so she and Christine would need to do some planning if they were going to make some memories that Lynette would never forget.

So that night, rather than sleep in her room, Wendy went to share a bed with her best friend. She and Christine talked late into the night about Lynette's upcoming birthday and some of the things they could do. It seemed like Wendy had only just fell asleep when their mother was waking them and telling them to get out of the house quickly.

"The house is on fire. Get dressed and get out quickly. The truck is parked in the road—go get in it," Cora told them. Then she quickly left to get Lynette up. While Wendy jumped into her clothes, Christine grabbed all the blankets off of her bed and her new saddle and they both headed for the door. Once outside they headed straight for the truck and climbed in. As Wendy looked around she saw the entire garage engulfed in flames. "Where's Sue?" Christine said as she opened the door of the truck.

"Here Sue...here Sue!" she cried. The little dog came racing out of the garage just as a big beam fell from the top. If Christine hadn't of called him when she did, he would not have made it out alive. That got Wendy's mind racing. She looked around for other dangers and noticed the goat shed was not too far from the flames. So she left the truck and worked her way over to the shed, released the goats and led them out into the larger field where they would be away from the fire.

"The fire trucks are on their way" Mitch told Cora. "The whole roof is smoldering and I couldn't save the cars. The garage is gone and soon the side of the house will be on fire" he was trying to stay level headed, but Cora could see the panic in his eyes. "I don't know if they will be able to save the place even if the fire trucks get here within the next few minutes."

"Well, let's save what we can," Cora said.

When Wendy got back to where the truck had been, it was gone. It was then that she saw Mitch pull it up to the front door and was loading out the piano with a man she had never seen before. A few other trucks were beginning to pull up near the door and folks were gathering what they could and loading up.

Christine came over and stood by Wendy and together they watched the scene unfold as if it were a movie of some kind. Trucks pulled up to the door, filled up with what ever they could grab and hurriedly left. It took only a few minutes before the entire house was emptied of all its larger furniture and the family's most treasured items. The helpers had told Cora and Mitch not to worry about their stuff and that they would be in touch. Just to stay safe and get what they could out before the structure burnt to the ground.

When the fire trucks arrived, they stopped entry into the home and made everyone stay at a safe distance. They went to work with their axes and hoses. Yet when it was all over, the garage had burnt to the ground, the end of the house where Wendy's bedroom was had been severely damaged, and the entire roof would have to be replaced. Three cars had been burned up, along with all the items that had been stored in the garage. Mitch's hunting gear and ammo, all the family photo albums, art supplies, two deep freezes full of meat, swimming pool equipment, a majority of the horse tack, tons of other treasures that had been temporarily stored, Wendy's favorite rabbit, and a box of baby chickens had all been lost in the fire. Yet at least no one had been hurt. All the animals were safe— except the rabbit and chicks lost in the garage—and the main part of the house had been spared. Wow! It was so hard to believe that this was really happening.

It wasn't long, however, before the insurance company came in and began repairs. Before the family knew it the building was nearly back to normal and a new garage stood in place. The yard was newly landscaped and a few more trees added. All in all, things looked even better than they did before the fire; however, family spirits were low as several of the members had been strung out all over the place, staying with friends and family while their home was restored. Routines were non-existent, communication was sporadic, and stress levels high.

Mitch decided the family needed to get away for a bit. Even though it was still wintertime, he decided to take them on a trip into Canada. Cora had always wanted to see British Columbia, and he thought that they might even want to live there someday. So the journey was scheduled and the family was soon on their way; however, the trip was short lived as a freak storm blew into the Northwest from the artic. When blizzard conditions hit with a vengeance on the fourth day, and temperatures dropped into the minus 40's, Mitch turned the car for home. Pushing his limits, Mitch drove long hours trying to get back home. The storm seemed to follow them, and they reached home in the wee hours of the morning on the seventh day. Icy winds cut through them like a knife when they climbed out of the car.

A light skiff of snow had dusted the ground and the crew left footprints as they walked towards the house. When Mitch reached for the doorknob, he quickly yanked it back as it nearly froze his hand. Using the end of his coat sleeve to hold the knob, he slid the key in and opened the door. It was dark and cold inside and the power had gone out. While Mitch went to flip the power switches, Wendy and Christine went to check on the animals.

On their way to the barn the girls passed by the swimming pool. It was covered with ice and there was frost covering everything around it. "Wow. This must have been some storm. I can't remember ever having one this cold hit before, especially not the end of March," said Christine. As she talked her breath made smoke like rings that drifted up and slowly dissipated. Wendy laughed and made smoke rings herself as she answered her sister with a

"Whoa...ho...at...did...yo...ou...sa...ay?". Chuckling, they watched their breath as they ambled over to the barn.

Although the animals had a warm place inside, the water troughs were frozen over with at least a half-inch thick of ice. The water faucets were all frozen too, so the girls spent the better part of the morning bucketing water from the house to the thirsty animals.

When they finished and re-entered the house, Mitch had a fire going in the fireplace. He had the television on the channel ten news and was sipping on a cup of hot chocolate. "Looks like this storm is going to be with us for a while'" he commented as Wendy and Christine sat down with hot chocolate of their own. . "The weatherman says it is going to last for a couple of weeks. It might even bring in a fair amount of snow," he paused before continuing. "Maybe we should cancel plans for Lynette's birthday party."

"Oh Dad we can't!" cried Lynette. "All my friends are really looking forward to it and I really really want a party Dad…please Dad….please…" she begged.

Against his better judgment he gave in. The party was still going to happen, even if the storm hung around. The family needed a pick me up and the trip sure didn't turn out the way he had hoped. Besides, he could use a good visit with the neighbors. It had been too long since the family had been together for something other than work detail, or recovering from disasters. Maybe they would break into that blackberry wine that Cora was brewing in the closet and play a few cards. So after a few words with Cora, preparations began to ensure a memorable time for their oldest daughter.

CHAPTER 20

Horses are Everything

CHRISTINE WAS TALKING
to Wendy, asking her if she was all right. "Oh, sorry Christine. I
was just remembering…" Christine gave her that "I understand"
smile and asked her if she was up to a ride. "Of course!" Wendy
replied as she raced her sister to the barn.

Oh the horses! Those wonderful creatures that tugged at your
heart and soul. They brought so much pleasure into your life… Yes,
pleasure, adventure, and entertainment… and now there were fifteen of them! Some were Quarter horses, some Thoroughbreds,
some Arabians, some Tennessee Walkers, some Mountain ponies,
and others "Heinz 57" variety. Some were young and unbroken,
while others were well trained. Most loved attention, but a few
wanted nothing to do with people. There was the old crew, Robin,
Tiki, Gigolette, Bandy, Queen Patron, Melody and Tonka. And the

more recently acquired, Mariah, Lady, Trinket, Daiquiri, Tequila, Taffy, Lightening, and Sugar.

Sugar was a grand old Connemara pony, an old mining breed, which taught all the children in the neighborhood how to ride. She was twenty-seven when she was given to the family and she was thirty-eight when the family gave her to some friends. The last they had heard, Sugar had a foal at forty-six and was in the newspaper since that would be equivalent to a 120-year-old woman giving birth! It kind of reminded Wendy of one of the Bible stories of Abraham and Sarah.

And Lightening was earmarked as a present for Grandma Mary. She was also in foal to Bandy, so soon there would be another foal forthcoming. It should be a nice foal; only this one was not going to belong to Wendy. She missed her little Shazam deeply. Even though she was now comfortable that he was waiting for her in heaven, she still wanted a baby of her own to play with. Someday she would try again for one. But now...now riding was the thing that brought her pleasure. Gathering up her bridle, she headed for the corral to catch a horse.

Choosing a mount to ride was always a pleasure with so many to select from. Each provided their own source of entertainment, as all had unique personalities and habits. Yet, even though the girls took turns picking horses to ride and play with—their favorites were Wendy's Robin and Christine's Tiki.

Over the next several months, the two girls rode every inch of the hillside owned by Brenda's rich father. They were never bored, as they were always doing something fun with their horses and friends. They made jumping trails, swam in the river, grazed the meadows, and just enjoyed lazing around on their backs. They rode on packing trips, in parades, in 4-H fairs, rodeos, and other community events. There were games of dude ranches, knights in armor, ladies in distress, cowboys and Indians, gold mining, cattle rustling, you name it…what ever the adventure…the horses were there to take them!

On one of their trips onto the hillside, the girls ran into a loose donkey. Where it had come from, they did not know. When it spotted the horses it ran over to say hello. At first its loud brays scared the girls mounts, and they tried to run off. But after a little bit they calmed and wanted to sniff noses with the new comer. When the girls went to leave the donkey followed. Deciding that they should not leave it to wander alone, the girls let it follow them home. When Cora saw them entering the driveway with the animal, she quickly stepped outside to the front porch.

"Now what in the world are you two doing with a donkey?"

"We found him mom," Christine said. "Can we keep him?"

"Of course not Christine! He belongs to somebody. Where were you when you found him?" The girls explained where they had found the little grey beast and soon Cora was on the phone with a neighbor trying to find out who may have lost a donkey. Within a couple of days the owner came and claimed his property. Loading the little guy up into the back of his pickup, he drove off waving and saying "Thanks."

CHAPTER 21

Favorite Memories

WENDY AND CHRISTINE
were sorry to see the donkey go, but when Brenda brought a pony
cart by a few days later, the girls completely forgot about him.
Christine immediately began to hook up contraptions for Tiki, so
he would learn how to pull the cart without hurting himself or
someone else. First she put a breast collar around his chest and ran
a long lunge line from the collar, through the stirrups on the saddle
and back to an old tractor tire on the ground. Then she did the
same thing on the other side. Yet, when she started to lead Tiki, he
saw the tire dragging behind him and he bolted. The young horse
was sure that the ugly thing was after him and it took three trips
around the back pasture at a dead run before he finally slowed and
realized he wasn't going to get eaten.

After giving the tire a good sniff, Tiki was comfortable. He let it drag behind him without further incident. So Christine hooked up another set of lunge lines for driving reins, then jumped up on top of the tire and let Tiki pull her around the grounds. She thought it was kind of like riding a chariot. Wendy laughed, but then took a turn and decided this was a pretty good idea after all. Next, utilizing the stirrups again, she hooked up a couple of brooms and ran them down each side then tied them to a short wooded pole at the back. This was to simulate the cart frame so Tiki would be familiar with something hitting his sides as he made turns and trotted around.

Before long the little buckskin horse was pulling the new cart like a champ! Up and down the roads he would trot with his passengers laughing, singing and just plain enjoying the sights. Christine and Wendy had so much fun that they would look for opportunities to hook up the cart and go for a spin. They also took great pleasure in delivering freshly baked pies to neighbors just to get a chance to play in it and had loads of fun giving the neighborhood children rides.

Then Cora told them about an upcoming local parade. She thought that maybe they should get the whole crew together and ride as a band of Indians. That was all it took. Preparations quickly began, neighbors were recruited, old history books were referenced, costumes were made, and an official entry submitted. Within a couple of weeks a team of fifteen girls rode their way onto Main Street for the Emerald Empire parade celebrations kicking off their local county fair.

They had made their costumes from gunnysacks and items they found around the farm, such as chicken feathers which they used in their handmade headdresses and tied in the manes of their horses. A few pieces of old leather and beads were tied together to make interesting pieces of jewelry that hung from some of their necks and costumes. Using brightly colored water-based paint, they had drawn circles around their horse's eyes, and placed handprints and stripes on parts of their bodies and legs. They had built a travois that a big dun-colored horse nicknamed "Buck" now pulled with two younger children aboard that held a small goat. Various fur coats bundled up to look like wild furs, and baskets of fruits and vegetables and other such items also rode on the travois. The rest of the crew rode their horses bareback with most of them only using hay strings for bridles.

The only mistake they made was taking a young stallion with them. As it happened, one of the mares was in season, so the team had to constantly move their horses around to keep the two horses apart and avoid any mishaps. This actually worked to their advantage as the people who lined the streets all thought the riders were completing a native dance drill of some kind and they really liked it. So much so that the band of Indians won the trophy for most authentic! Wendy would never forget that adventure, especially since she was the one who got to go up to the stage and collect the award. A photographer took her picture, which now was tucked away in her secret place where she stored all her most valued treasures.

A funny memory was when Uncle Robert brought two of his Air Force buddies visiting. They were both from Russia and had never ridden a horse before. So when the girls offered to take them riding they were game. They told Uncle Robert that two little girls couldn't get them into too much trouble…after all riding horses wasn't like flying jets, now was it; however, when they returned from their trip a couple of hours later, two pale faced men covered in dirt and all beat up and bruised climbed off their mounts. They could barely walk. Addressing Uncle Robert and Cora, they simply said "We should have known we were in trouble when the girls asked us if we wanted to take the running trail or the jumping trail." After learning that they weren't seriously hurt, only bruised and sore, Uncle Robert ribbed them unmercifully about two young girls getting the better of two strong fighting men. The two "tough guys" had gained a whole new appreciation for the "little girls!"

Another favorite memory of Wendy's was the Fourth of July pack trip. Mitch and Adrian loved to fish in the high lakes, and did so on any occasion they could. They decided they would take the entire family to celebrate the Fourth. So without too much ado, they arrived at Waldo Lake with enough equipment and horses to supply a small army. Nine horses and riders along with two pack-horses headed down the thirteen-mile stretch of trail towards the high lake called upper Eddie Leo. Seven walkers trailed by two milk goats followed behind.

Most of the walkers were kids that preferred to hike rather than ride, but a couple of adults brought up the rear. Wendy rode in the back keeping an eye on the walkers with the goats. She enjoyed the trail as it was not only beautiful, but offered something interesting around nearly every corner. Wendy not only saw beautiful mountains and valleys, but she also witnessed a beaver working on a home in a large pond that they had dammed from a spring fed creek, as well as a huge bull elk that stepped out onto the trail unafraid of the horses and curious about the goats. She saw a waterfall, several beautiful rocks that she would have to stop and collect for her growing pile on the return trip home, and a couple of huge meadows with lush green grass covered in brightly colored wild flowers. Her heart soared!

By the time her trek ended at camp, the men had already

removed the packs and set up cooking tables and placed tarps on the ground for sleeping bags. There was no tent, but then it was July, so sleeping out under the stars was to be the mode of operation.

Betty and Cindy were busy preparing sandwiches for the hungry travelers, while Uncle Butch and Robert were constructing a bathroom—complete with a bucket with a toilet seat on top surrounded by a teepee like wooden pole structure wrapped in black plastic. They had even taken a stick and slid a roll of toilet paper onto it then tied the stick to one of the poles.

There was a wonderful lake that peeked through the trees just beckoning the young to come take a dip in her, or to try their hand at fishing. Wendy took a deep breath and soaked in the sights. Then she dismounted, tied her horse to the rope strung between two large fur trees where the other horses had been tethered, and removed her horse's saddle. Joining her sisters, she helped roll out sleeping bags and began gathering firewood. David, Caleb, Joshua, and their friend Kevin, turned their attention to the three rubber rafts and fishing gear, while Mitch hung lanterns in strategic places around camp. Mitch also set up a fire pit complete with grill for the coffee pot, frying pan and other cooking needs. Later he would roast his marinating chicken over the grill along with the corncobs he had brought along.

Adrian helped Cora build a small pen for the milk goats, while Grandma and Nina set up the cooking area, setting out cooking pots, and large bowls for heating water, utensils, and dish towels. They also set out a homemade cupboard packed full of several canned goods and other food stuffs to be used for later meals. A tablecloth was placed on the camp table that had been built by previous campers and now sat in the center of their campsite. A

lantern was placed in the center, along with salt and peppershakers, a couple of decks of cards, some bags of chips, and some candy bars. Three large ice chests were placed in a shady spot to help keep them as cool as possible. When the workers stopped, the campsite was very comfy.

It didn't take long for the boys to put the rafts and fishing gear in the lake and try their hand at catching trout. They didn't have to wait long as the trout were hungry and the worms they trolled behind their rafts were too much for them to pass up. Soon there were enough trout for three days worth of meals! The boys were so happy with themselves that they started bragging about who caught the biggest and most. Over the next several days more than fifty fish were caught! Some were gratefully eaten while others were kept in the coolers for later consumption.

Wendy, Christine, and Mitch were on one of the rafts trolling in the middle of the lake when they spotted Uncle Butch yelling, jumping up and down, and frantically waving his arms at the camp shoreline. They couldn't tell what he was saying so Mitch rowed closer to see what he wanted. As they reached earshot they heard the words BEAR! Mitch rowed faster and when they hit the bank, Butch nearly jumped in with them. It was hard to tell who was more scared, the black bear that had mistakenly entered camp or Uncle Butch!

Wendy never saw the bear, but Uncle Jim had caught a glimpse of it fleeing when Butch had run for help. Several of the horses had spooked and broke their tethers, running off down the trail at high speed with Betty, Cora, Cindy, Anna, and Grandma in hot pursuit of them. Although the bear had caused quite a stir, he never showed his face back at camp again and after a good laugh, the campers settled back into a routine.

The girls took turns grazing the horses in the grassy meadows and swimming them in the lake. Some picked wild huckleberries, some explored, others fished, and still others read, took naps or played cards. They all shared in waving sparklers on the night of the fourth while Grandma served fresh huckleberry pie. Umm… umm did that ever taste good!

Everyone agreed that the goats had been a great idea, as they provided fresh milk that was used in cooking, or placed in the lake to cool for later drinking. It didn't seem to matter what time of the day it was; you could hear laughter and contented murmurs from all parts of the campsite.

Then the rain came. In a mad dash, the adults ran for plastic. Anything was fair game as they frantically attempted to cover bedding, clothes, and other items that might be damaged by a good soaking. The sleeping quarters had successfully been covered just as the downpour hit. Since it was nearly time for bed anyway, folks just snuggled into their bags for the night. Yet the rains didn't let up. For most of the night the rains came down, leaving the entire campsite muddy, wet and cold. The plastic had leaked above Wendy's bed and she was soaked to the skin along with Christine.

"Mom. Mom I think it's leaking over here. Are there any dry bags?" Wendy asked.

"Sorry Wendy. There are no more bags. You'll just have to stay where you are." Then she reached over and felt the sleeping area near Wendy and Christine. "Oh my goodness! You're soaked!'" she cried.

"That's what I was trying to tell you Mom," Wendy replied starting to shiver from the cold. Christine woke up as Cora began to shuffle around. "Eew… I'm wet…" she said. "And it's cold!" "Here" Cora handed her a dry pair of sweats to put on. Getting out of bed the three girls tried to secure the plastic so no more rain would come in. But it was too late for the bags.

Mitch got up and tried to start a fire, but there was no dry wood. That's when others in the camp began climbing out. "Well" said Adrian. "Our bags are wet too. Maybe it's time to pack and head home." Grandma Mary started breakfast over the camp stove. At least there was still gas so they could have a hot meal. "I agree with Adrian," she commented. "It's been fun, but this wet and mud is more than I bargained for." Other such comments followed from more of the crew, so it was decided that they would prepare to leave.

Wendy would never forget those special times. The good, the bad, and the hopelessly funny…

CHAPTER 22

The Accident

WENDY HAD BEEN DREAM-
ing again when Christine awoke her and asked her if she wanted
to go for an early morning ride. The past few weeks had been filled
with work, everything from picking beans and strawberries to hay-
ing for a little extra cash. The girls were saving up for winter horse
feed and more riding equipment. She stretched as she climbed
out of bed and reached for her blue jeans. After dressing, she met
Christine in the kitchen for a quick bowl of cereal then the two
headed up the road for their mounts.

The horses were up the road at Grandma Mary's place. The
grass had been cut for hay on their twenty acres, so Grandma had
let them put the horses in her field to help eat the tall field down.
Besides Lightening and her filly, Bonnie, who was now almost six
months old and wilder than a March hare, were lonesome with-

out the herd. At least that is what Grandma claimed. Wendy had been helping her for the past two weeks doctor Bonnie's hind leg. The young filly had cut a gash on the lower part of her pastern but was too wild for them to catch and doctor. Wendy had told Grandma that she thought they could tie Lightening to the fence, then gently walk the filly beside her mom—cornering her between the fence and her mother. Then someone could reach under the mares belly and spray the healing ointment. It had worked like a champ, Grandma standing at the back of the mare and the filly thinking she was cornered stood still as Wendy reached under her mother and sprayed the wound. Grandma was very grateful for Wendy's help.

Looking at the filly right now, Wendy thought that one more spray job would take care of the problem, as the wound had healed completely over and was now mending quite well. So she caught Lightening and headed for the fence. Wendy told Christine she would be with her in a few minutes that she wanted to help Grandma one last time. Christine headed off to go catch Tiki while Wendy led Lighting up to the fence and tied her, Bonnie following behind. Like normal, Wendy hollered over the fence towards the house for Grandma. When she turned back around, Bonnie had moved over in front of her and stood about six feet away. Suddenly the filly turned and kicked out at Wendy catching her in the jaw with both hind feet.

Wendy saw stars and the next thing she knew she was picking herself up off the ground. She could feel the swelling of her mouth and numbness started seeping in. It felt like all her teeth were gone and blood was pouring from her mouth. She crawled under the fence and headed for Grandma's front door. Grandma had heard Wendy call and was just opening the door to come out when Wendy reached it. One look at her face brought a cry from Grandma's lips. Her mother, Elizabeth, was visiting and she came to the door to see what the problem was. Elizabeth immediately took control, having Wendy squat down. She gently held Wendy by the shoulder, soothing her while Grandma Mary ran to get a towel. After giving Wendy the towel for her face, Grandma Mary called Cora. Within minutes Mitch and Cora were in the driveway with the car. When Mitch removed the towel from Wendy's face, he lost it.

"Oh my God, its hamburger!" he cried without thinking. Cora saw the horrified look come over Wendy face. Giving Mitch a look of "careful what you say buster" she turned to Wendy and let her know everything would be fine. It wasn't as bad as her Dad had said. But once the three of them were in the car, Mitch drove like a crazy man for the hospital. Wendy prayed that God would give her strength to deal with this.

Grandma Mary had all ready called ahead to the hospital, so they were waiting for them at the emergency entrance. Wendy was immediately whisked into a room where she was to meet a plastic surgeon. "Dr. Copeland is the best plastic surgeon on the entire West Coast," the nurse told Wendy.

"Hello" said the Doctor as he pulled on a pair of rubber gloves and began to check out her face. Wendy was terrified and was sure now that she had no teeth left, but she didn't cry. She might have lost it, but Cora and the nurse were so calm she was able to control herself.

The Doctor left the room telling them he would be right back. Wendy leaned over a bowl that the nurse had for her and let some blood and saliva run into it. She finally got brave enough to ask her mother if there were any teeth left. It was hard to talk and when she tried she could barely understand herself. But somehow her mother understood and assured her that she could see all her teeth, that Wendy probably just couldn't feel them because of all the swelling. It was then that Wendy realized her face was now completely numb—probably why it no longer hurt so much.

Dr. Copeland came back into the room and spoke with Wendy, assuring her that he could patch her up to where there would be very little scarring. He had a camera in his hands and took several pictures of her face. Then he told her he didn't think her jaw was broken; however, she had several loose teeth that he may not be able to save. He would do his best, but a couple of them had been broken off at an angle—right where she took the brunt of the hit. "I want to send you to x-ray to make sure your jaw really isn't broken," Dr. Copeland said. "Then we will get you into surgery, before your face can do much more swelling." Turning to Cora, he asked her if she could step outside for a minute.

Wendy said a quick prayer and surprisingly a peace settled over her. She couldn't explain it, but knew The Lord had to be watching over her. She was no longer afraid at all, for she knew in her heart that He would be with her every step of the way. She also knew He would be guiding the Doctors hands in surgery. "I have to cut your clothes off now," the nurse was saying. "We cut them off as we want you to move as little as possible." Then she took a pair of scissors and cut off Wendy's shirt and jeans. Thankfully she left her underwear alone. She then helped Wendy get dressed in a hospital gown and put a funny little paper shower cap on her head.

The x-rays went quickly, but it took a while before they actually rolled her into surgery. Evidently the Doctor had needed some old photos of Wendy to see what her face had originally looked like, so Mitch had been sent back home to retrieve them. They had to wait for the photos, so now Wendy's face was even more swollen.

It was nine hours before they brought Wendy out of the surgical room. Recovery took another hour, but Cora was there when Wendy woke up. "Wow! You do have a few stitches there my dear,'" she said. "And you're going to have one pretty bruise on your face for a bit, but the Doctor did an outstanding job. The nurses are all saying that his work is so good, it is almost like he was signing his signature." Wendy tried to speak through her now very swollen lips, but nothing came out. Cora continued, "The Doctor says you can come home in the morning, but they want to keep you overnight for observation. Your surgery took longer than they expected, and they want to make sure there are no complications from the anesthesia." "Will you be staying with me mom?" Wendy tried to ask, but still nothing came out. "I'm sorry honey, I don't understand you. You're just mumbling. But I thought I would stay until you went to sleep, then I would go home and get you some clothes, since they cut up your other ones." That brought a chuckle to Wendy's lips. But it really hurt. "Besides" Cora went on, "The nurses are really nice as you have seen, and they assure me they will take good care of you. But I'll stay all night if you want me to." Trying to be brave, Wendy tried to let her mom know she would be fine. But again, she could not talk.

Cora found a piece of paper in her purse and gave it to Wendy. She wrote that it was Ok for her mother to go home...she would be fine and she was really tired anyway. Handing the paper back to her mom, she closed her eyes and was soon fast asleep.

When Wendy opened her eyes, Cora was sitting beside her with a book. The clock on the wall read 10:10am. "You're awake!" Cora said with excitement in her voice as she closed her book. "Did you sleep well? Boy, I had a hard time not waking you. I so badly wanted to show you what I brought!" She quickly picked up a bag that she had on the floor by her feet and began pulling out items. She pulled out a western shirt—pink in color with golden threads woven into the cotton material. It had a herd of colored horses running across the front and back yolks. "Oh! This is beautiful!" Wendy wanted to say, but only grunting noises came out. Her mother smiled in acknowledgment and pulled out a stretchy white skirt. "I thought this might be easier to get into for the trip back home," Cora said as she continued to pull items from the bag. Out came a new pair of blue jenes, pink socks, and a bra.

Wendy's face flushed bright red. Even though she was almost fifteen, her development was slow and she hadn't needed a bra; however she secretly wanted one because the girls at school were beginning to make fun of her, calling her Twiggy. Even her older sister had said she was flat as a board. Wendy looked up at her mother in adoration. Cora answered her look with "A mother's intuition."

As Wendy sat up to put her new clothes on, she spotted a mirror from across the room. Looking up she saw herself for the first time since the surgery. She gasped and all the color drained from her face. Well, not all the color… there was plenty of black and blue and purple… She looked like Frankenstein's monster! She reached up to carefully touch this face that had somehow grown to more than three times it's normal size. Wendy would have cried right there if her mother had not once again come to the rescue. Gently touching her shoulder, Cora told her "I know it looks bad right now honey. But don't you worry any. It will all go away in a couple of weeks. The swelling and bruises are just part of the healing process." Trying to be brave for her mother, Wendy let herself believe she was right and focused on getting dressed. But she was visibly shaken.

The Doctor came in for a final check then signed the release papers so they could leave the hospital. He handed Cora some papers with instructions on how to care for the wounds until the stitches came out. "I'm sorry but they must be cleaned every day. The better they are cleaned, the less scarring there will be. The stitches on the inside will all melt away anywhere from ten days to two weeks. The ones on the outside will have to be removed in about three. I've taken the liberty to schedule an appointment for you." Cora asked about food, and he told her that she could only eat soft foods for a while. Her mouth will tell you when she is ready for more solid things. I sewed in her front two teeth, but I am not sure they will live, and I'm pretty sure she is going to have to have those two lower ones removed as soon as she can handle it. They have broken at an angle so they won't be able to be saved. I would have pulled them, but I didn't want to add any more trauma to her jaw right now. She needs to do a little healing first. Oh, and she must have complete bed rest for at least a couple of weeks." Turning towards Wendy and looking her right in the eye, "That means you'll have to stay put so that you don't get dizzy on me and collapse. You have been through a lot young lady and even though you may feel ok, you need to give your body a chance to rest and heal." With that he gave Wendy a hug and assured her that she was the prettiest young lady and the bravest, that he had ever had the pleasure of meeting.

As soon as he left, Cora and Wendy headed for home. Upon arrival Wendy was taken straight to her room. There she found a brand new nightgown laid out on the bed for her, an adorable stuffed horse, some flowers from friends, and a whole bunch of get well cards. She would have to read them later though; she was feeling pretty weak and tired as she climbed into bed just as Christine came bouncing into the room. She stopped short when she got a good look at Wendy, but recovered quickly and grinned at her sister. "I'm so glad you're alright. I was so worried about you!" Cora stuck her head into the room and told Christine to give her sister a quick hug and then let her sleep. "I had to promise the Doctor we would give her plenty of rest in order to get to bring her home early. You can talk to her all you want later."

With that Christine reached over and gave her best friend a hug and that's when Wendy saw the tears. Wendy tried to tell her little buddy that it was ok…everything would turn out fine…but nothing came out. Not even mumbles." So she gave her sister a return hug and waived bye as she left the room.

Her strength was zapped. Without being able to stop them this time the tears rolled freely down her cheeks. "Lord, she said silently, this is going to be as hard on my family as it is on me. Please be with them and give them peaceful hearts as you have me. I know we will get though this and I thank you for all the love you have shown me. You're such a faithful friend." Then she was asleep again.

CHAPTER 23

The Recovery

The healing process took time and Wendy was getting impatient. It had been a little over two weeks now and she was getting antsy to get out of bed and do things. But her mother said she still had to stay in bed for another week. "Doctor's orders," it seemed was the excuse for everything now. Oooh! It was beginning to get on her nerves.

Yet, Wendy had never felt so much love in all her life. Her family was there for her every need, even bringing her a little bell that she could ring when she wanted something. Since she couldn't talk, they had brought her several notepads to write her thoughts, needs, and or wants on. They had also removed every mirror from her room and the bathroom, so that she didn't have to look at herself and worry. In addition, friends and family stopped by to visit, often encouraging her and letting her know she was missed. They wanted her to hurry up and get well so they could see her more often again. Well Wendy wanted to hurry up and get well too, but there were complications. There are always complications so it seemed…

She had no problem handling the daily cleanings. Even though it hurt, Cora was very careful and patient as she worked around the stitches keeping the scabbing away as the Doctor had instructed. Cora tried hard to be as gentle as possible and had even counted the stitches for Wendy—One hundred seventy one of them on the outside. She couldn't count the ones inside of her mouth, but the Doctor had told her there were more on the inside than the outside, hence the reason for the longer surgery time.

But what Wendy was having a hard time dealing with was the eating. She had lost so much weight she thought she was going to drift away. And she was getting weaker rather than stronger with the weight loss and complete bed rest. She was also hungry all the time. But she couldn't eat very well because of the broken teeth. Cora had been giving her diluted baby food, which Wendy had to basically pour in her mouth, then tipped her head back and let it run down her throat. She couldn't drink through a straw so it was a very slow process, again because of the broken teeth. Although the baby food helped take the hunger pains away, it wasn't giving her body all the nourishment it needed. In addition, Wendy could smell the real food coming from the kitchen and she could hardly stand it!

Again Wendy prayed for strength. And once again a peace settled over her allowing her to control her impatience and temper. Her anger in check, Wendy was able to return all the love she was getting from everyone else. In fact she couldn't remember ever having felt so loving before and she realized the feelings she was able to express had to be coming from The Lord himself.

Finally it was time for her appointment with Dr. Copeland. When he saw her, he was both pleased and worried. He was pleased with the healing of the cuts on her face, but worried about her weight loss. When Wendy got on the scales, she barely made 62 pounds. With her small five-foot frame, she was almost a walking skeleton. "Ok he said. Let's get these stitches out and then get you to a dentist who can remove those teeth." He was very gentle, but Wendy could feel every thread as it was removed. As soon as he was done he handed Wendy a mirror. "Those scars are purple now, but they will fade with time," He said. "And if they don't get light enough for you, then we can do a little more surgery later and make them nearly disappear." The way in which he told her, made her believe he could do almost anything. But for right now, Wendy was to let her body complete it's healing.

As Cora and Wendy left his office, they drove right over to the Dental building. Wendy was never so happy to see a Dentist in all her life. Although it was painful when he pulled the teeth, Wendy was glad to finally be rid of the broken monsters that had wielded so much havoc on her body. And finally, she could eat something!

They didn't even make it home before Wendy had talked Cora into buying her some solid food. Anything...Cora had to remind her that they would have to introduce solid food back into Wendy's life slowly...as not to mess up her system and cause even worse problems, but she finally agreed to ice cream. Within minutes Wendy was happily licking a vanilla cone that she was sure was the best thing she had ever tasted! Then after a week of going through soups and salads, then chicken and fish, Wendy had moved onto more substantial food items like steak and potatoes. Wow! She didn't know she could eat so much.

Wendy was picking up weight, although it came much more slowly than she expected. It took almost three months to gain twenty-two pounds. She felt much stronger, her energy returned, along with her smile. So she knew she was on the mend; however, there were still deep purple scars that faced her in the mirror everyday and she wondered how long she would look like a monster. Although no one else seemed to notice the mess on her face, the scars were all Wendy saw when she looked at herself in the mirror and it depressed her. She had always taken for granted the beauty that had run in her family. But now she was the ugly duckling and it hurt. Maybe a ride would help. She would ask mother in the morning if she could finally get back on a horse.

To her surprise Cora had readily agreed that a ride would be good for her daughter's spirits. She just insisted that she start with a real short one. Yet when Wendy approached Robin to climb on, her body froze completely up. She couldn't move. All of her muscles had locked up and she couldn't move in inch. Her heart raced wildly as she thought about her predicament.

"Hurry up Wendy, we're burning daylight!" Christine cried. But when Wendy still couldn't move she started to shake uncontrollably. That was when Christine realized her sister's extreme fear and tried her best to help her. "It's ok Wendy. This is Robin. Your favorite mare and she loves you like I do. She won't hurt you." That seemed to help as Wendy felt the muscles loosen slightly. "And remember, you don't have to do this right now. We can try again later if you want…" Wendy's mind stilled and the shaking stopped. In a few more minutes she was able to crawl up into the saddle. Once on her mares back, Wendy was fine. She took a deep breath and then chuckled. "I don't know what came over me. I just couldn't move Christine."

"That isn't surprising Wendy. You had quite an ordeal. Fear is a protective mechanism and it may take you several months to get over it. Give yourself a break!"

They kept the ride short as promised, mostly because Wendy was still a little weak, but partially because Christine was still worried about her sister's "frame of mind." But it was just what Wendy had needed and soon she was back to normal in both body and spirit.

As riding became routine again, Wendy had no more problems freezing up. That is once she was on the horse's back. When she was on the ground and a horse started jumping around, her body would freeze up. Yet it was sporadic, so Wendy never knew when it was going to happen. It really frustrated her, as she knew the complete healing process was going to take a lot longer than she had imagined. But Wendy was determined it wasn't going to stop her from loving and riding the horses.

CHAPTER 24

Endurance Racing

BY SPRING THINGS HAD
pretty much returned to normal on the farm. That's when Christine
began to share her desire to run an endurance race. She had just finished reading the Black Stallion series and decided she wanted to
run a long distance race—maybe even up to Canada! Christine was
sure their horses were every bit as good in the mountains as any others, and strongly felt that her and Wendy were already toughened up
from years of riding. Wendy was glad to embrace her sister's dream,
especially after the months of loving support she had just given her.
So the planning began.

Christine told Wendy that proper conditioning of the horses
was the key to winning. Hence they began their training by taking
loops around their twenty-acre field at a fast trot. Somewhere Christine had read that the trot was the easiest gait on a horse, sighting

that they could travel a much further distance faster, if they trotted rather than mixing walking and galloping. Next the girls timed their loops to see how long it took them to travel around the field. They got to where they could judge their speed with ease both in the field and over the hills. Christine would then compare their ride times to a chart showing the Tevis Cup results. The Tevis was a one-hundred mile race that was run in Northern California and was World renowned by endurance racers. If they could get close to those ride times, they knew they could win.

As the days went by, they added a little more distance to their rides until they were riding over twenty miles a day. When Cora found out what they were doing and how much progress the two had made, she had to get in on the action. Cora was not only supportive, she wanted to join them! It was with Cora's help that the girls learned that there was a lot more to running a long distance race than just covering the miles.

The hardest part was finding a good mount with a trainable mind and solid feet and legs. If the hooves weren't strong they would break down over time and lame the horse up. The same held true for the legs. Any natural faults caused problems the more miles you put on the horse often preventing you from continuing in the race. The horses mind was also critical. If the horse didn't like to get out and travel, or if it didn't travel well with others, it could quickly put you out of competition. Luckily, Christine and Wendy's horses were of strong sturdy stock and had excellent feet and legs, and they loved to go! Cora however, had a little more trouble finding a horse that met their criteria.

As the miles continued, the girls learned how important it was for their horses to be able to recover quickly. Meaning their heart rates and breathing had to return to normal within a certain period before a vet check would allow them to move on. A stethoscope was purchased and each one learned how to take the horse's pulse at rest and at work. With their local vet's assistance they learned how to optimize their horse's workouts and recovery.

Doc Miller also taught the girls about electrolytes and how important they were to keep the horses from dehydrating. They learned what type of feed was best to give to hard working horses, and what type of equipment worked best. A hackamore without a bit, a light weight saddle that allowed the horses back to breathe, and a pad that protected cinches and saddles from rubbing yet gave the horses some cooling ability were all very important.

Rider's equipment was equally imperative. Therefore each of the girls carried lightweight saddlebags full of food, water, and treats for the horses. They also tied a rain slicker, an extra rope, and miscellaneous goodies such as a hoof pick, a rubber boot in case of a hoof injury, a pocketknife, and the like to their saddles. Wendy called it a "survival kit." Then to protect themselves, they wore nylons under their blue jeans so blisters wouldn't rub their knees, a light cotton shirt, and tall boots to also protect the calves.

After many months of riding and training, the girls decided to try their luck with a twenty-five miler. Cora signed the three of them up for a ride up near Three Finger Jack. Things got really exciting when preparations began for the haul up to the race site. Once there, Cora checked them in and got their ride numbers. They unloaded the horses and settled into a camp spot for the night. With a couple of hours to go before dark, they took their horses out to scout a bit of the trail and catch some light exercise. After taking the edge off the horses, they headed back to camp to prepare for the next day's race. It would start promptly at 7:00 A.M.

Wendy awoke with a start. Glancing at her wristwatch she

noticed it was only a little after four in the morning. She rolled over and tried to go back to sleep, but sleep evaded her. Her thoughts were on the upcoming race and how she thought it would play out. Finally she got up and checked on the horses. While giving them each their electrolytes and breakfast, Christine came up to help. "Can't sleep either?" Wendy asked her sister. "No. Too much to think about and I'm too excited," Christine replied. "Here, let me help."

"Where's Mom?"

"She's still sleeping, but probably not for long…"

Sure enough, Cora had herd the girls talking and was soon up bringing them something to eat. Before long the entire race facilities was bustling with hopeful riders preparing for a ride and looking forward to a bit of fun. At 6:00 A.M., the loud speaker crackled with a "Good Morning Riders!" and then began reciting the days planned activities. When seven o'clock rolled around, the first horses and riders were released from the initial vet checks to begin their official start down the trail. There would be three vet checks along the way and each horse and rider would be timed in and out of each. Times would be totaled up for an overall race finish time and riders would then be announced in order of their finish. Awards were to be presented to the top five with the best ride times, and the top five horses in the best condition.

By the time Wendy was called, it was almost nine. The clock lady told her she was the sixty-sixth rider to start down the trail. Cora was right behind her and Christine was following her. They let a horse and rider go every two minutes. When the clock lady said go she gave Robin her head and they started trotting down the dirt pathway. Robin was feeling really spunky, so Wendy knew it would be a very good day.

Within minutes Cora and Christine came galloping up behind

her. They slowed to a fast trot as the three shared the trail together. It was beautiful and the weather had cooperated. Cool, crisp, yet dry. The horses felt way too good and looked for boogiemen behind every tree. Snorting and feeling like a keg of dynamite, the horses had to be held strongly to prevent them from running off. Even though the girls weren't worried about them going twenty-five miles, this was their first ride and they wanted to make sure they had plenty of horse left when the time called for it.

Then a rider came galloping from behind and ran right passed them. Wendy had a really difficult time keeping Robin from bolting. "Whew!" said Cora. "She was in a hurry. Hope her horse—" As she was speaking a second rider came racing past them in a full out run.

"Whoa! Maybe we are supposed to run," Christine piped up. The three looked at each other, smiled and then let their horses go!

Wow! Was this ever fun! It felt much like their normal rides in the hills around home, only at a faster pace. By ten, the three of them had made it through two vet checks and had passed over twenty horses. So they knew they were making good time. Then they came to a really steep hillside where they saw two riders in front of them, off their horses and tailing them from behind. Christine and Wendy jumped off and started to tail their horses. Cora said "Nuts to this" and continued to ride her mount up the steep hill. After about a third of the climb, both girls jumped back on top their horses, deciding it was too much work walking behind, even if the horse helped drag you up.

At the top of the hill they learned why riders had climbed off their horses. There was another vet check. So before entering they took a few minutes to let their horses recover their breathing and get their pulses down. The tough little mountain ponies that Wendy and Christine rode, passed with flying colors. But Cora was held back. She told them to continue on without her; she would catch up down the trail. Heading out the girls soon discovered they were headed back down the other side of the steep mountainside. At the bottom they found a wonderful creek that they took time to let their horses swim in. Back on the trail, they passed another set of riders and horses. A little before eleven they rode into their last vet check. There was still no sign of their mother, so the two girls rode on.

With this being their last leg of the trip, Christine and Wendy decided to race for the finish. So they kicked their horses into full gallop. They crossed the finish line with Christine about four horse lengths in front of Wendy. Both were laughing hysterically and their horses still wanted to run. Dancing in place, Robin and Tiki were officially checked in by the clock lady. Laughing with them she said, "Well, looks like you two had fun!"

"Sure did!" the girls replied in unison, which brought even more laughter.

"OK. Head on over to the last vet check for your final check through," she told them. Dismounting they led Robin and Tiki over to be checked out. After approved, they went to their campsite and bathed and fed their mounts. There was still no sign of their mother, so they walked back to the reader board to see if they could get some news. According to the board, Cora had left the last vet check about ten minutes behind Christine and Wendy. So she should be coming to the finish any moment. The girls ran over to the trail and sat and waited.

Cora came around the corner and into sight riding alongside a young girl. They crossed the finish line together. Evidently, Linda, that was the girl's name, had been dumped by her horse when he spooked. Cora come upon them, stopped to make sure she was all right, and then help her catch her mount. The two completed the last leg of the race together. That did not surprise either Christine or Wendy, but it brought a lot of arched eyebrows from the race officials. Not too many people stopped their racing to help out another rider. They were normally left to their own—unless of course the life of horse or rider was involved. Cora was a heroine of sorts. At least to Linda she was.

Later the girls learned that out of one hundred and twenty eight starters, Christine had finished eleventh in two hours and seven minutes, Wendy twelfth in two hours and eight minutes, and Cora sixteenth in two hours and twenty-two minutes. A special treat for Wendy was that Robin had also won fourth place for best condition. Although secretly Christine had hoped to win, the three girls couldn't be happier!

At home that night, they had much fun relating their experiences to family members and showing off Robin's fourth place award. All the girls could talk about for the next several weeks was the race. They had been quite surprised to learn how fast everyone had run in the twenty-five-miler, as nothing they had read had prepared them for that kind of speed. They also had learned that as the distances became longer—fifty miles or more—gaits of the horses, tailing ability, and other such things became much bigger factors. In addition, they had learned about electrolytes and other vitamins, minerals and products that aided in the horses ability to recover quickly and keep from dehydrating. They learned about equipment and clothing that provided more stability and comfort and discussed all kinds of new strategies. The more they talked about strategies, the more they wanted to plan their next race. After all, they all knew there would be a next race... and Christine had BIG plans...